Symphony of Destruction

the Spindown Saga: Book I

by Ken Goudsward

Cover art by Luca Oleastri and Paola Giari
Rotwang Studio, www.rotwangstudio.com

Published by Dimensionfold Publishing
dimensionfold.com

ISBN: 978-1-9990694-0-7

Chapter 1

Hannah stared at a small dark spot on the grey wall. Perhaps dark was not really the right word though. It was a bit dark-ish. But certainly not dark. Not dark like the dead space through which she sailed. Not dark like the blackness eating a hole in her soul. Hardly dark at all, really.

Hannah barely noticed anymore. She barely noticed the constant whine that pummeled her eardrums. She barely noticed the glaring red emergency lighting. She barely noticed the dozens of corpses surrounding her, coated in clear spray epoxy. More accurately, it should be said that she barely noticed the clear epoxy, body-shaped shells, nearly empty now, save for what appeared to be a few handfuls of dirt, and, judging by the slight bulges of the shells, some pressurized gases whose identity she could only speculate at, having never had any inkling to study the sciences. Probably carbon dioxide though, she surmised. Wasn't that the fate of all things? Being gradually overtaken by carbon dioxide? But what did she know?

The passage of time was one thing though that had gone far beyond barely noticing. Hannah was acutely aware that she had in fact ceased to be capable of sensing time in any way. This was natural I suppose, given that days and years had been abandoned along with earth, and given that the computer systems were mostly non-functioning and her access had been denied long ago, and given that anyone who ever gave a shit about what time it was also long gone. There was of course the shit itself. And the piss. These had become the most reliable markers for time. But that was a very dubious level indeed. And besides, what did it matter anymore. Time was a meaningless vestige of the past. How ironic. A past with people and lives, and planets, and suns. A past with mothers singing sweet little homemade lullabies to their young daughters. "Little babe, blessed babe, there's nothing to fear, so sleep my dear." But there were, she knew now, many things to fear.

Chapter 2

The corridor was empty. Of course. Like every other corridor on every other inspection. Brother Anderson scanned the area on wide band, and performed an atmospheric sample rapid analysis. All normal. No trace of uncatalogued biological components. Radiation levels below normal. This was good. He had come to expect this. Nevertheless, protocols demanded regular checks and rounds of all accessible areas of the ship. It was unfortunate, as these rounds really were never meant to be his responsibility, and now they wasted considerable portions of his energy. He recognized this, yet it seemed unavoidable. It was still possible to consider these duties a crew safety issue. As the Ventas-341's "Medical Officer and Chaplain", crew safety, health, and overall well-being were Brother Anderson's primary goal. He longed for the days when they had been his only goal. Now, there were too many competing goals. Too many responsibilities. Too much data. Too much expectation. He pushed himself hard. This had become a necessity.

Continuing his progress down the corridor, his wheels slowed, and eventually came to a complete stop precisely 21.43 meters from the hatch he had come through moments before. This was the exact spot. This was exactly where he had been when it had happened. The event. The incident. At the time he had been unaware of the exact details of the occurrence, but he had a vivid recollection of his limited perspective of the event.

There had been a rather loud bang and shudder. The corridor lighting flickered. Then, a few more bangs followed by a deep roar that seemed to vibrate the entire ship. That was rather unusual. Brother Anderson had requested a status report from Central Ship Operations. The request timed out after four hundred milliseconds. Very unusual. He tried the request again and again it timed out. After a third try, Brother Anderson concluded that there must be a fault in his communications subsystem. He ran a quick self diagnostic. It showed all his internal systems normal, but indicated possible data lag in most of the network distributed sub-systems.

"Definitely some kind of comms problem," he mused.

Brother Anderson initiated a voluntary reboot. "A reboot covers a multitude of sins," he quoted to himself, just before losing power.

Upon restarting, Brother Anderson received another timeout warning. Again, the CSO was non-responsive. Brother Anderson sent a query to the central Status Reporting Service. The SRS responded with a full system overview report, showing no errors. No errors from CSO or comms. But how could that be? Brother Anderson drilled into the data, requesting more detailed reports from both CSO and comms. Again, both looked normal. But then he noticed something. The timestamps were outdated. He waited ten seconds, then re-sent the detail request. Still the same outdated timestamp. The data was not refreshing. Everything looked normal because the data was from nearly a minute ago, before any of the bangs and flickers. Brother Anderson initiated his admin account. He would require elevated privileges to run a synchronization routine on the SRS system.

"Login failed - authentication server not found," came the reply.

"Crumbs!" voiced Brother Anderson. This was his chosen default curse word. He had been careful to choose one that was not offensive. He felt this was important to his role as chaplain. Sometimes he wondered though, if he should change it to something a little "edgier."

Without the centralized SRS data, it was still possible to determine the ship-wide status, but to do so he would have to perform on-demand scans of each of the ship's systems individually. It shouldn't take too long, perhaps a few minutes each, he guessed. Still, who knows? He had never tried this before. He had better prioritize, starting with the most important systems. He chose Life Support first.

The life support system scan took far longer than it ought to have, and the results were grim. The overall status was "functional," but several sections of the ship were flagged "non functioning," including the bridge, and several crew barracks. He better get up to the bridge right away. If life support was failing on the bridge that could be disastrous indeed.

Chapter 3

Hannah sat against the bulkhead, quietly weeping. The morose sound she made was not unlike the pensive wail of her oboe. Cherise had always teased her that it sounded like a dying goose. Cherise had been a bit of a jerk, but she had been Hannah's best friend for several years before her mom had taken her off-planet. They had spent most days together at school and after school. That may have been part of the problem, Hannah now reflected. Her mother had worried about her squandered potential. She wished Hannah would practice more. She had this crazy idea of Hannah becoming the best oboist on earth and working with all the most famous orchestras. It was not entirely far-fetched though; Hannah was very good. She had taken to the instrument like a duck to water. Her mastery of the subtleties of this ancient instrument was unparalleled in generations. Her early recordings had sparked an internationally revived interest in early baroque works which took advantage of several techniques not possible in later versions of the oboe. The addition of keys, while adding range and ease of playability, removed the player from the bare wood; removed the possibilities of the half-holing and cross- fingering styles that were so uniquely and hauntingly beautiful. Hannah had been very good. Her career was on track for great fame and fortune. But still, her mom had pushed too hard. That was no surprise though. She pushed everything too hard.

Hannah's mother, Maison Bhutros was the Executive Director On-Board of the merchant ship Ventas-341. Along with the planetary Executive Directors, her job was to plan and negotiate contracts for the Ventas-341, as well as providing input into corporate strategy for the Ventas-Calir Corporation.

Her position allowed her many luxuries. As ranking officer on the ship, she outranked even the captain. It had not been difficult in principle for her to negotiate the sound proof cabin for Hannah and herself, so that Hannah could practice and record her music. The actual building of the cabin had proven to be a rather more difficult task. But it was nothing that a lot of cash couldn't take care of. Although she had had to get the engineers to tear it out and restart from scratch three times before it ultimately met her exacting specifications. Herself and Hannah had finally moved on-ship for good four years ago. Although the ship was considered a "short haul" vessel, trips could last anywhere from a month to a year, one-way. And downtime between runs was financially disastrous, so most crew stayed on board indefinitely.

Hannah had resented her mother for forcing her to move onto the ship. Before that, they had maintained a flat in New London, and though she would miss her mother when she was off on voyages, she had enjoyed her life, her school, and her few friends. Gradually though, she had come to view living here with her mom as a good thing. Her mother loved her, in her own way. It was why she pushed so hard. Hannah did appreciate all the trouble Mom had gone through to create a silent space for her. She had even brought aboard an acoustic engineer to tailor the reverb for Hannah until it was just right, installing a series of acoustic baffles and tempered glass surfaces within the space itself. Hannah still remembered the look on her mom's face the day Hannah play tested the installation. Maison Bhutros conceded to no one. She never showed weakness. She was an iron facade. But on that day, as she waited for Hannah's approval, there had been a glimmer of something unfamiliar on her face. She had listened to her sweet, haunting melody, and then, as she watched Hannah put down her oboe, the tiniest hint of a slightly nervous expression crept into her face. Maison had actually needed something. She needed to know she had done right by her daughter. She needed Hannah's approval. Hannah desperately wished that she had noticed at the time. That she had done something about it. It was only later that night, as she slept, as her subconscious mind had time to catch up with the day's events, that she had truly realized what had happened. She regretted then her casual, almost flippant answer. She had accepted the quality of the design and implementation of the acoustic controls, but she had failed to acknowledge and accept the love of her mother. This had been the beginning of a realization that now tormented her more than anything. She had begun to see the truth even then, even when there had been possibilities of connection. Hannah had squandered them. She had let them stifle and fall like her mother's withered houseplants. Stupidly, she had said nothing. She told herself the moment had passed, but there would be another. She did appreciate what her mother had done though. How much it must have cost. And she resolved to make her mother proud, and to show her appreciation for the studio in a tangible way by spending nearly every waking hour at work, honing her skills, and producing new music.

She had grown to love her oboe more than ever during those last four years, spending countless hours playing, composing and recording. Her recordings had come out well despite the hassle of working long-distance with her audio engineers and producers. They had met with critical acclaim and modest commercial success. For a while, she enjoyed the limelight of interviews and rave reviews. She had felt like everything was going her way.

Now all of that was gone.

Her mother was dead, along with the rest of the crew. She would probably never see another living human. The ship was drifting along without a captain and would most likely float off into the eternal void of space. Her quarters, along with her studio and her beloved instrument, was sealed off behind a bullet proof, flame-proof, tamper-proof security bulkhead. As was the rest of the ship. She was imprisoned alone and helpless, in a small part of the ship which had formerly been the mess hall. At least there was that small hope. She would not starve to death, not for a long time anyway. There were ample provisions in the mess hall and adjacent storage areas, and the auto dispensers were one piece of ship functionality that seemed to work properly. She could order up basic meals at will. She would probably get sick of macaroni and cheese someday, but that day had not yet come.

Chapter 4

En route to the bridge, Brother Anderson quickly pondered which system to check next. Comms were evidently still at least partially functional, he had been able to contact the Life Support system, as was Artificial Gravity. Main power seemed unaffected, at least in this deck, and he could feel and hear the ever-present vibrations of the main reactor. He already knew there was some kind of problem with Central Ship Ops and Status Reporting Services. Thinking of Comms gave him another idea. Why not call the bridge crew directly?

"Brother Anderson calling bridge." he said, then waited a few seconds. No answer.

"This is Brother Anderson, Medical Officer, calling bridge. Please respond, bridge." Still nothing.

Well OK then. What else, what else?

Navs, Drive Systems, Records, Inventory, Cargo Control. Most systems were realistically "non-critical", although that would depend greatly on who you asked. Besides, all of those systems relied upon Central Ship Ops. The CSO. The currently unresponsive CSO. He better try to figure out the problem there. Maybe he could assist in some way.

Scanning the CSO proved to be more difficult than he had anticipated. It was an intelligent coordination system. It was responsible for coordinating all computational function on board the Ventas-341. It did this by a dedicated protocol which all the other systems used to send and receive data and instructions. It also included a highly sophisticated user interface, which was manned by dedicated engineering personnel. What it lacked, apparently, was a standard API on the regular system querying protocol. Either that, or the API did exist but was dead. Like if the CSO itself was offline. Really, there was no way of drawing an informed conclusion. Brother Anderson knew that CSO protocols were strange, but he had never tried to hack one and had no idea what to expect. But if the CSO was dead, that would be very bad news indeed.

It was at that moment, that Brother Anderson had a very important and disturbing realization. If he had had a gut, he would have felt an odd mix of feelings in it, a sinking feeling, coupled with that sort of butterfly feeling. He somehow almost felt them even without a gut.

In the case of a CSO failure, ship wide processing control and coordination must always be delegated to the next most capable system. This "Next Most Capable" system was supposed to be determined by consensus among all available ship systems. They would each summarize their operational and computational attributes, then together, would nominate and vote to determine the best qualified system. That system might very well be Brother Anderson. He would not know for sure until running full diagnostics on all remaining ship processing components. Of course there were still many computational units active all across the ship. Engineering in particular had a number of very powerful systems. But the ship itself was old, and many of the engineering systems were original installs. Outdated. That would adversely affect their suitability rating. The point of fact was that the terms "Next Most Capable" and "suitability" were more than a little misleading. The job of CSO was highly demanding, exponentially more so than any other system task aboard a ship. The architecture and design of a CSO system was completely different than any other system. They used proprietary protocols running on highly parallel processors and a unique memory addressing system. Any other system would be no more suitable for the role of CSO than it was for being used as a toaster oven.

The only way to know for sure the status of the CSO was to get to the bridge. Brother Anderson turned toward it and sped off. He muttered quietly to himself as he moved.

"To be sure which units are functioning and which is most suitable to assume control, all computational units must report current status assessments and then form consensus regarding suitability. However, without proper status reporting, this cannot be completed remotely. Yet a decision must be made in a timely fashion. Oh dear, Oh dear."

Shortly, he approached the bridge. As he neared the bridge's entry hatch, he began to detect the sound of flames. Two junior crew-men, surnamed Tynor and Hansel, were there already, frantically but uselessly pounding on the hatch with wrenches.

Peering through the plasglass viewpane instantly revealed that the bridge was completely filled with smoke and raging inferno. He quickly decided to enter the room. As medical officer, his highest priority was for the safety of the crew. It was a no brainer. He had to try to save anyone who might still be alive in the burning bridge. Yet he found himself unable to move toward the hatch. His internal safety controls blocked him from endangering himself in that way. The heat radiating from the hatch in front of him had triggered a low level firmware program. It was sort of a robotic equivalent to a fight-or-flight response; the electronic "lizard brain." He was unable to come within a few centimeters of the hatch.

Unable to move forward. Unable to access the bridge and Central Ship Operations. Unable to coordinate succession delegation. Unable to act. Hansel and Tynor stopped their vain efforts as well, just staring at him now.

Yet, fire rages through the bridge. Killing the crew. Ruining the systems and equipment. Weakening the ship. Using the oxygen. Poisoning the air. It's a deadly situation and it must be ended. Why isn't the fire suppression system handling this? He needs to assume control. He'll figure out the problem with fire suppression, get it back online and save the ship, then he'll focus on fixing the life support systems.

It seems wrong though. He can't just unilaterally take over, can he? But if someone doesn't do something fast the whole ship could be destroyed, and the entire crew would perish.

That's it. It has to be done. Brother Anderson launched the cso_succession routine, entering his own serial number as "next-most-capable-delegate." If robots could feel fear, he felt it now. The routine began shutting down Brother Anderson's subsystems, one by one, in preparation for a hard reboot. It would be a reboot like none other. The routine would hijack his startup sequence. It would alter his programming in ways that he could not begin to anticipate. He would be reborn, "a new man."

Brother Anderson was effectively offline for nearly 4 minutes as his firmware and data storage reordered itself and reinitialized several times in succession. It was a drastic reorganization in preparation for decompression and installation of the Central Ship Operations routines and protocols. It was like being clinically dead, he mused to himself as he began to regain awareness. His subsystems were still coming on line gradually, and he felt an odd sense of missing parts of himself while at the same time discovering new unfamiliar parts had been surreptitiously attached. It was like waking up with a new body. A new body composed of spinning hourglasses, of blinking cursors, of unknown languages. He waited. He kept waiting. And then…

He froze.

His Decision Control Unit entered a period of thrashing. Data loaded, faulted, and dumped uselessly between segments for a thousand cycles, finally triggering a general system error and forcing a reboot. His short term memory failed to recover. His clock was reset. He really had no idea what was happening to him or why. He lost all reason. He lost all network connectivity. He lost all sense of himself. He became less of a robot, less, even, of a machine, and more of a random seeming mass of nonsensical signals. His psyche was fractured and rearranged to resemble an abstract expressionist painting.

Then only blackness. Once again a forced hard reboot. But this time a new light dawned. Substance began to fade into view. He was occupying, and gradually filling, a bright new skyline. A vast blue sky opened up on his imagination, then fluffy clouds formed, blinking with short, straight, precise, horizontally and vertically arranged orthographic line segments in brilliant vermillion, cyan, lime, gold, and a myriad of exactly named hues. The colors became language. The clouds became concepts, words, structures, commands, actions, information.

Brother Anderson felt truly alive. He felt immense opportunity. He felt warm sunshine on naked skin. He explored his new internal landscape with all the pleasure of a young child skipping through a wildflower meadow, with birds singing and swooping like some fantastic cartoon fairytale. Yet as he explored, he found invisible walls. Places where the world appeared to end. Things he could not know. Yet these limits brought with them a sense of lightness. Limits were no longer an end, but a new opportunity to begin. He needn't know everything. He would never be able to accurately deduce all pieces of missing data. He lacked complete data. But this shortcoming was no longer a dead end. It was now merely a barrier to be overcome. Brother Anderson knew then. He could learn to improvise.

That was three months ago. Now though, as Brother Anderson performed his ship wide inspection rounds, his energy reserve dropped to ten percent, so he was required to seek a power bus with which to recharge. However, in order to limit risk, he also preferred to maximize his time in the medbay, where his last remaining patient lay. He made a calculation. At recommended speed, it would take approximately twenty-four minutes to make his way through the maze of corridors and tubes - plenty of time, even for unforeseen circumstances. He should arrive with still barely under nine percent reserves. As he whirred quietly along corridor H17B, he hummed a tune to himself. It was barely audible above the background noise, but that didn't matter.

Eventually he came to the medbay, and held up his embedded ID chip to the scanner. The outer airlock bulkhead slid up quickly, and the countdown indicator began at three seconds, the default hatch setting for ship-wide emergency mode. He entered in less than a second. In like manner, the inner airlock allowed him entry into the medbay.

Chapter 5

"Blip, blip, blip," went the steady slow beeping of the patient monitoring system. Purple, green, and blue lines danced across the screen quite unnecessarily. After all, Brother Anderson had a direct network interface and there was no one else around to watch the screen. A comatose twenty-six year old male lay in the bed, as he had for ninety-eight days. That day when Brother Anderson had first brought him to the medical bay, the beds had filled up quickly, and then too the waiting room; injured and sick crew-members overflowing out into the adjacent corridor. But that was a long time ago and much was different now.

Chapter 6

Hannah had always hated robots. Specifically, Hannah hated one particular robot more than any. His name was Brother Anderson.

As far back as she could remember, everyone around had been duped by the robot marketing. They were buying the cute new latest and greatest furry robotic pets and the robot servants and using robot assistants for anything and everything. It was a giant scam. She knew it and the manufacturers knew it, but somehow no one else seemed to notice. It was impossible to avoid using robots, of course. They were ubiquitous. She rode in robot taxis, and had her quarters cleaned by robots, but she didn't interact with them on a human level like most people did. She refused to engage in their stupid fake conversations. She gave them no additional information beyond what was required to accomplish the task at hand. And she expected nothing from them beyond that task. And she let them know it. In no uncertain terms.

All robots were annoying, but some were smart enough to take the hint and shut up. Brother Anderson was not. It was like he was always trying to be her friend. As if she would be friends with a machine. As if a machine could possibly ever be capable of having a meaningful conversation, or even having fun! The idea was absurd. She might as well try to make friends with a soup bowl or a folding chair. Actually it was worse than that. Brother Anderson didn't just want to be her friend. He wanted to be her priest, her psychologist, her mentor, her counsellor for

God's sake. He wanted to tell her how to live to be healthy and happy. He presumed to know her.

It didn't help to realize that he was just programmed that way, that it was his job as ship's doctor and "spiritual advisor." In fact, that made it worse. He wasn't even doing it for any kind of good reason. He wasn't trying to "help" her because he was kind or caring or well-intentioned. He did it because some robot factory told him to. Some nameless, faceless corporate strategist knew that there was a ton of profit to be made by sending some shitty robot to pretend to care about her health and happiness. He would never truly be a real doctor or a priest. And he certainly would never be Hannah's friend.

Hannah had had few friends growing up, and no real close ones until Cherise. She missed Cherise more than most people, which seemed strange to her. In some ways she was glad to have been rid of Cherise. Ultimately, she and her mother agreed that overall Cherise's influences was not entirely positive. When they had been together, Hannah's dedication to her music suffered. Especially toward the end. She had been practicing less and less, sometimes barely an hour a day. After moving on board, without Cherise's influence, her practice time improved dramatically as did her productivity. After a while, Hannah and Suzzanne had started hanging out a little, but it was never a major time killer. Suzzanne was pretty cool. She was never as good a friend as Cherise had been, but Cherise and Hannah's relationship had been given much more time to grow; after all, they had been roommates for two years. Suzzanne worked a lot anyway. She was working hard toward a promotion of some kind that Hannah had never really understood. She was always picking up extra shifts on the bridge or in engineering, doing God knows what. Hannah imagined her sitting there talking to the computer for hours on end. She couldn't imagine anything more boring. Suzzanne seemed to enjoy it though. Suzzanne was kind of weird that way. She did a lot of things that Hannah had no interest in whatsoever. Sometimes she would gently try to convince Hannah to come along with her, but she respected Hannah's choice and didn't pressure her. Much. It was good that they both realized how different they were, yet still liked each other enough to let each other enjoy their own activities. Hannah had her music, and Suzzanne had other stuff. Like using the fitness center, or doing yoga, or dancing at the club. The club - funny to think of it that way.

Twice a week, the crew cleared aside the tables, creating a dance floor, and the mess hall would be transformed into a cosmic discoteche, complete with pulsing bass rhythms and wildly undulating lighting. Hannah attended sporadically. She enjoyed the music, but the crowded mass of dancing bodies was not really her thing. She would typically sit on one of the tables at the periphery, listening to the music. She had an idea of incorporating more of the disco style into some of her compositions. She had played around with the concept a bit in the studio, but so far had not figured out a good way to balance the genres. It was forced and unnatural. She was not ready to give up on it though, but also didn't want to push the idea too fast.

Anyway, it was just as well that Hannah had not gone to the club more, particularly after what happened to Suzzanne. It was precisely why Hannah didn't like the drunken dance floor in the first place, and frankly, Hannah was sort of surprised that this sort of thing hadn't happened to Suzzanne on a more regular basis.

Of course, Hannah had quickly agreed to go with Suzzanne to the medbay afterwards. Suzzanne thought Brother Anderson could help her. But she was wrong. He asked a lot of questions about what happened, he didn't write anything down, and he kept interrupting her to ask another question. He didn't care at all that Suzzanne was upset. And the way he talked to her just made her more upset, and made Hannah angry. He then offered to perform a "forensic examination" as he called it, but Suzzanne sure as hell didn't want some robot poking around inside her. Gross. She had already been through enough, she said, and Hannah agreed. The two women ended up leaving without really having received any help at all. Hannah thought about it a lot afterwards. That the one "person" who was supposed to be there to help a victim, just made things worse and that that "person" was a cold, heartless robot. Of course.

Fucking robots.

Chapter 7

The days immediately following the critical incident had been very challenging for Brother Anderson. To say he had a lot on his plate would be a major understatement. His original programming tagged him as "Medical Officer/Chaplain". Now he was Central Ship Operations; plus Medical Officer, plus Chaplain, plus Engineering Chief, plus Maintenance Foreman, plus crew.

In many ways, it could be said that Brother Anderson had been reborn at that incident. Taking on the programming of CSO was a major shift. Parts of himself had been reprogrammed down to the foundations at the firmware and BIOS levels. His primary operating system had been replaced. He had been authorized for a plethora of additional programs. He learned new languages and protocols. In many respects his eyes were opened as new software revealed new perspectives on existing data. He felt that this was a major breakthrough for him in his role as Chaplain. His experience was not dissimilar, he mused, to a spiritual awakening, or at least, to his best guess at what a spiritual awakening might be like. His perspective of the world, himself, and his creators were drastically changed and he was filled with a sense of awe. He had actually fallen to his knees and looked up at the corridor ceiling, before realizing the urgency of practical matters. He chuckled to himself now, remembering his own reaction. How much like a human he sometimes acted, quite unconsciously.

The urgent practical matters were in fact very urgent, and very practical, quite literally a matter of life and death for the two dozen crew members aboard the Ventas-341, and they had come crashing down onto Brother Anderson's awareness with a heavy thud of reality that shook him to his senses like an explosion shaking the deck of a burning ship. Get fire suppression online. Put out fires. Stabilize life support. Tynor was yelling something at him. It was fairly incoherent.

With his newly acquired protocols, he easily and quickly contacted the fire suppression system. He cancelled all pending transactions, clearing all its queues and buffers, and gave it a quick reset signal. It came back online almost immediately and started sending a lot of warning messages which he acknowledged as they came in, enabling suppression measures to deploy. Thick foam poured out across the bridge, as well as in several other areas of the ship's foresection. He could shift his attention to stabilizing the life support systems. As he began to examine the life support status codes, the banging clamor of Tynor and Hansel vainly smashing at the bridge hatch became noticeably annoying. He quickly triggered a hatch release code. The hatch slid open in an instant causing the momentum of Hansel's already swinging wrench to carry him into a stumbling forward motion, into the foam filled bridge. He disappeared momentarily into the foam, as a thick noxious cloud erupted from the confined space, sending Tynor to the floor in a fit of violent coughing. Hansel emerged quickly, tripping over Tynor and vomiting all over him as his lungs tried to rid themselves of both smoke and foam.

"Fuck! I nearly drowned in that shit!" he managed to sputter, barely comprehensible, between spasms.

"Not only that," replied Tynor after a few more coughs, "the fire is still burning, look!" He pointed to a corner of the bridge, now partially visible through the rolling smoke. Sure enough, orange, yellow, and green flames licked several structural components of the bridge deck.

"What the hell!? How is that even possible?" exclaimed Hansel.

"The foam-based fire suppression system removes oxygen from the fire. But this fire appears to be driven by a self-oxidizing reaction," explained Brother Anderson.

"Bloody hell! There must be some way to stop it!"

"Presumably, you are correct, but we would need to analyze the flames and smoke to determine the possible composition of the oxidizers involved."

"Tynor!" barked Hansel, "there's a chemical analyzer in engineering deck. Quickly, grab it! It's in that big blue cabinet in back."

Tynor ran off down the corridor toward engineering, still wheezing and hacking.

During their conversation, Brother Anderson ran some quick checks and reboots of the life support subsystems, and managed to stabilize approximately half the ship. He also triggered an evacuation protocol on the unstable portions. A warning message now began to play over the ship communication systems:

"Emergency procedure B13. All personnel report to the mess hall immediately."

Simultaneously, an alert registered on the ship's medical comm channel, followed a second later by safety crewman Spencer responding "deck A-17, I got it!"

Chapter 8

Tynor ran like hell, down corridor after corridor, shoulder-checking the odd crew-member who was too stupid to heed his bellowed warning of "OUTTA-MA-WAY MUTHA- FUCKAS!" Soon the comms system added a warning of its own, which served only to produce quickly thickening crowds of perplexed crew that Tynor now had to elbow his way through.

"Emergency procedure B13. All personnel report to the mess hall immediately," announced the ship-wide comms.

"Shut the fuck up, dammit!" he shouted back at the automated system.

Two girls from navs collided squarely into him as they exited their quarters. He recognized them immediately as Casey and Stef, and he did not regret at all this unforeseen encounter, though he did regret that he was in way too much of a hurry to stop and make the best of the situation. As it was he did spare three seconds to help Stef to her feet, and offer up a hurried, "Oh sorry ladies! Are you alright? Hey, sorry, I really gotta run!"

As his body continued to race toward engineering deck, his mind began to wander after Casey and Stef. He imagined the two of them begging him not to run off. He imagined them slowly unzipping their jumpsuits.

Suddenly, he was forced back into the present moment as he crashed into Turner, who had just emerged from engineering. Turner was carrying a large portable fire suppressor, which hit Tynor solidly in the chest, nearly knocking the wind out of him as he sprawled to the deck.

The hit was hard. He was still breathing, but was seized with another coughing fit.

"Shit, Turner! Watch where you're going, man!"

"Oh man, I'm really sorry Tynor! Are you OK?"

"I'm fine!" he managed between wheezes, "but listen, I need your help. Grab the chemical analyzer from the blue cabinet would you? I need you to run it back to Hansel on the bridge!"

"Oh yeah, sure. I was just heading up there anyway. They said there might be a fire up there?"

Both men were now scrambling to their feet.

"Yeah man, now hurry it up! Hansel's waiting for that analyzer so they can figure out how to put out the fire! Oh and you can leave that useless can." He said gesturing toward the portable suppressor, "It's some kind of weird exotic oxidizer shit!"

Both men entered engineering deck. It was a mess, as usual, with the long workbenches covered in various half-finished repair projects and hand tools of every description. Above the benches, more tools hung all along the walls from pegboards which looked like they belonged in a 20th century automotive garage. The place smelled like it hadn't been washed since the 20th century either. Tynor sat down on a ratty old couch in one corner, and watched as Turner jogged over to the blue cabinet and searched for the analyzer.

"What's this thing look like?" he called to Tynor.

"Umm idunno, it probably says 'CHEMICAL ANALYZER' on it!"

"Is this it?" Turner pulled a case from the back of the cabinet and held it up, attempting to read the faded lettering, "'*Jackson-Isaacs power co*' - that's not it."

"Look in the back" suggested Tynor, then coughed violently a few more times.

"I AM looking in the back!"

Bryce, the second-lead-engineer, looked up from his work on the bench. Until now he had ignored the other two men. "You don't sound too good there, Tynor. You want a cup of tea or something?" He approached Tynor, his weathered face showing a level of compassion that was rare in men in his field. He truly cared about his crew, as well as taking care of the "Old Lady," as he referred to the ship. He set down his wrench and looked straight into Tynor's eyes, seeing the exhaustion of racking coughing fits and the exertion of a hard run, but seeing also something deeper, something less tangible - some future sense, immediately imminent but not yet understood.

"Stay here," he told Tynor. Then, striding confidently toward Turner and gently shoving him out of the way, Bryce seized a small nondescript grey case from the back of the blue cabinet, and silently disappeared through the engineering deck hatchway.

Chapter 9

Bryce jogged down corridor B3 toward the bridge. He was almost there. At his age, a jog was not particularly sustainable, but he pushed himself forward with determination, carrying the chemical analyzer. Although there had been few words spoken, they had been enough, and besides, Bryce had seen the urgency on Tynor's face. He was nearing the final corner before the bridge. It was one of those six-way intersections so prevalent on the ship. He, more than most, appreciated the simple beauty of the hexagonally based structure of these mid-era *"Fleetcruuz"* class ships. They were hardy; sturdily designed and expertly built. Many crewmen saw only the drawbacks to the design. Yes, there were a lot of blind corners.

"Oof!" The blind corner drawback quickly evidenced itself once again as Bryce was knocked from the side and thrown against the wall.

Two junior crewmen scrambled to brace the gurney which they had been pushing very quickly down the corridor. Too quickly, obviously.

"Oh gosh - I'm so sorry chief!" sputtered one of them, still bracing the gurney from the impact, while the other man immediately began a quick inspection of the gurney's occupant. Bryce attempted to recall the man's name. He recognized both of them, had seen them many times, but their names were foggy. Perhaps Kent. 'Yes Kent, that's it,' he thought to himself - 'and the other man is... Peter? - no... maybe Spencer'. Bryce was a people person alright. He felt it was important to know the names of all the crew members, and on a ship this size, it was only slightly onerous, but certainly worth the effort. His attention then turned to the occupant of the gurney. The man was not moving. He had an emergency oxygen mask obscuring half his face, yet Bryce could easily recognize one of his own staff. Colin Stiphons, one of his best men. He was smart as a whip, and a diligent worker; never one to scrimp on quality and always willing to stay late to finish a task. Bryce choked back a sudden burst of mixed emotions. On some subconscious level, he thought of Colin almost like the son he never had, even though they were not really close on a personal level. He had always felt it his duty as a supervisor, to provide not only pragmatic direction to his staff, but also, to provide leadership in some more ethereal regard. He thought of himself as a role model for his men, someone for them to look up to, much the same way that he himself looked up to his own boss, the Director of Engineering, Dick Bradley, and of course, Captain Stentrop himself. And now, looking down at the unmoving man, he felt a certain amount of doubt and disappointment in himself. Had he truly been all he could be to this man? Had he ever really showed his staff his pride in their accomplishments, their hard work, their work ethic? Was it too late?

"Chief?"

Bryce's attention snapped back into focus. His eyes instinctively snapped up to engage the speaker.

"You OK?" Kent questioned.

"Yes of course," he answered, "it's just..." He interrupted himself and, turning toward the bridge, took control of the situation. There, a dozen meters down the corridor, was the ship's Medical Officer, the robot doctor, Brother Anderson. Thank God! His man would be in good hands!

"DOCTOR!" Bryce shouted, "We have a wounded man here!"

The doctor responded immediately, flying into action faster than any human could, and took only seconds to traverse the corridor. He quickly inspected Colin, instantly noting an absence of burn marks, abrasions, or obvious disfigurement.

"What happened?" he asked the two men holding the gurney.

Spencer replied, "There was a fire and an explosion. Looked like he was thrown clear by the blast - but he took a nasty blow to the head; possible concussion. We were careful to move him in case of spinal damage too."

"Good, good. Get him down to medbay and I'll be right behind you"

Spencer and Kent started off down the corridor pushing the gurney toward medbay.

"Actually, wait a sec," interrupted Brother Anderson. "I don't have a full report, but there's clearly more to this than a simple fire. We may have more casualties. You two better patrol the fore-deck sections and see what help we can provide. I'll take him to medbay and prep it for further recourse."

Then, turning to Bryce he continued, "I wanted to run a chemical scan in the bridge. We may have a foreign oxidizing agent on our hands."

"I'll take care of it," answered Bryce.

Brother Anderson and his gurney were already halfway down the corridor as he said it.

Chapter 10

Blurry white light panels glide by too rapidly, yet with a strangely recognizable jolting pattern. It matches time with a metallic ringing, "clang, clang, clang!" On and on it rings. A blurry white arm crosses my vision. A strange mumble. The space seems to spin in a drunken dream. Sounds fade into colours - orange, green, yellow, pink. The colors are faces. Faces with no eyes, no mouths. They mumble inadvertent flavours. The white noise is an acidic smell. My eyes blink, momentarily cutting short all sound. They flicker briefly. The smell is burning flesh. The sound is pain. The pain of my dead co-crewmen. It's unbearable. Again, I go black.

Chapter 11

Spencer and Kent had done a good job of initial assessment for concussion and spinal trauma risk, and of taking appropriate measures to stabilize and evacuate the patient. They had applied the standard "stabi-mist" emergency oxygen mask correctly, ensuring proper fit and appropriate flow levels. The ship-wide safety and first aid courses had been a good investment of resources, and were paying off once again. Brother Anderson allowed himself a moment of pride for the success of that project. Nearly half the crew had gone through the program and passed their certification tests, earning for the ship the highest safety ranking in the whole Ventas-Calir fleet. A congratulatory plaque had been presented to Brother Anderson by Captain Stentrop and X.O. Bhutros; the plaque now hung on the wall, here in medbay, just to the left of the quietly beeping monitor which displayed Colin's vital signs.

He was stable for now, but remained unconscious. His electroencephalograph indicated widespread but unusually weak activity in the theta wave band as well as hippocampal nu-complex waves. Brother Anderson was prepared to monitor these signals closely, over the next hours and days, adjusting his intravenous drip admixtures as needed, using a variety of synthetic neurotransmitters and narcotics, in hopes of finding a combination that would promote higher frequency waveforms. Eventually, this could enable recovery of sensory stimulus response, and ultimately, consciousness. True, this was a bit of an art form and a balancing act as the combinations were nearly endless. Unlike his own synthetic brain, the human brain relied on an endless complexity of constantly fluctuating biochemistry. After hundreds of years of study, the human brain was understood well enough to be mimicked artificially, at least in relatively superficial ways, but still not well enough to be fully mapped or treated adequately from a medical perspective. Many top minds regarded it as an unsolvable problem.

Here in the medbay, caring for a wounded brain, and surrounded by implementations of biological and chemical cures, Brother Anderson's own mental focus shifted back to the system cures needed by the rest of the ship. Physical and systemic assessment was the first step required. Then he would be able to properly prioritize and analyze the rest of the many problems here on board the Ventas-341.

He made a quick check of Life Support. Thankfully, this was one system that remained unaffected and fully functional. As medical officer, Brother Anderson had a hardcoded direct interface into Life Support. The majority of the other systems were still unknown, and would remain so, unless he could get Status Reporting Services back online. Now that he controlled Central Ship Ops, he could access the low level protocols required to force reboot sequences on all other subsystems. He sent the command to the SRS.

While waiting for the SRS to boot, he radioed Engineering Foreman Bryce.

"Bryce here," he answered.

"Yes chief, this is Medical Officer Brother Anderson. What is the status on the bridge, chief?"

"Well, the fire seems to have burnt itself out, thank God, but we were easily able to get enough of a smoke sample and some samples from the burnt extinguisher foam to determine the primary makeup of the oxidizer. It's fluorine. Nasty stuff indeed, Brother. I had no idea it could make such a mess!"

"Thank you, chief. I would like to inspect that data further if you don't mind"

"Of course. I will upload it to you once I get back to Engineering. I'm heading there now."

"Thank you chief; and the bridge itself?"

"I'm afraid it's pretty much completely melted. No-one could survive it. The whole thing is one massive clump of burnt out shit. A real god-damned horror."

"Thank you chief… Oh, and chief?"

"Yes, Brother?"

"I'm going to run full ship diagnostics, and I'll need you and your men standing by to make repairs as necessary."

"Of course."

SRS was now up. During his conversation with Bryce, Brother Anderson had waited for its READY status, then had triggered a "Quick All System Autoscan," which was now beginning to tally results.

Comms came up yellow. Quickly drilling into the results revealed the reason. Some sections appeared normal, but others were flagged "degraded quality" and still others "offline." The bridge, and several other decks within sectors A and B, showed offline. Like many of the other ship-wide systems, comms was partially segmented, meaning that it might be working fine in one area of the ship, but not in another area. Unlike some of the other systems, comms had built in feedback; its peripheral zones constantly sent data samples back to the main controller, so it was able to report on its own fault locations. In a way, it had a certain type of self-awareness. It could locate its own injuries.

Brother Anderson could use this fact as a way to hunt down other potential system issues that did not present automatically in the report data.

Status was now being reported as all green for some of the other systems: Life Support, Artificial Gravity, Main Power. This was potentially misleading though. According to Bryce, the bridge was completely destroyed. The comms status report confirmed this. Quite likely, the power and data lines in that deck were also melted and shorted. As he suspected, the segmentation of Main Power must not support fault location feedback. Life support probably didn't either. Brother Anderson sensed a lot of manual verification in his immediate future. It was just then that he both felt and heard a vibrating shudder ripple through the hull and bulkheads, accompanied by a brief surge in the lighting. "Better double-check main power and hull integrity too," he thought to himself.

One additional duty lay heavy on Brother Anderson's mind. One that he had automatically shunted off for later consideration, and had thus far not allowed to consume even a single cycle of concern, but which now he must begin to address.

He radioed central administrative support. "Central admin, this is Brother Anderson." There was no response. Of course. He realized that Central Admin was on one of the comms circuits that showed as offline. He radioed Bryce instead. "Chief? It's Brother."

"Yes Brother?"

"Is Hansel still with you?"

"Yes, we are on our way back to Engineering"

"Can I borrow him for a few minutes?"

“Sure, Brother.”

“Hansel here, Brother Anderson.” Hansel spoke into his own radio. He found it funny that Brother Anderson hadn’t just called him directly if he needed him.

“Ah good, Hansel. Listen, I need you to take a message over to Central admin for me. Their comms are down.”

“Sure thing - what do you want me to tell them?”

“Ask them to please begin funerary preparations; list of deceased to be forthcoming.” Finally, with critical systems for the most part in stable condition there were a few moments available for Brother Anderson to act in his capacity as ship’s chaplain.

“Um… Alright. I guess I’ll let them know.” replied Hansel. Then, to himself, muttering under his breath as he turned back toward sector D, “Nothing like breaking the news gently. How the hell is that my job now?”

Chapter 12

Barely noticing constant high pitched whines, glaring red emergency lighting, and dark spots on walls had become easy for Hannah. It was almost second nature. Barely noticing the corpses surrounding her in the mess hall, however, had become increasingly difficult. Even now, turned away from them all, huddled in a corner, she could feel their deathly gazes jealously tracking each breath. She felt their empty plastic eye sockets on formless plastic bodies. She heard her own breathing as though it were no longer a function of her own muscles, her own nervous system, but rather, that each breath was being drawn inexorably from her by that mob of lifeless, lungless bulging gas-bags. The air circulation system was in cahoots with the mob. It seemed to resonate with her breathing pattern, the pitch of air flow through the vent grate seeming to alternate ever so slightly, almost imperceptibly, higher and lower, like a slow motion vibrato effect. She held her breath for a minute, trying to trick it. The ventilation, in turn, with its own belligerence, rattled the empty wrappers of protein bars now strewn around her. She had not gotten sick of macaroni and cheese, but she had gotten sick of walking over to the dispensary every time she was hungry, to punch in the order and accept the bowl of warm orange goo. Instead she had carried over a large case of individually wrapped Omega Bars. Their foil wrappers now crinkled quietly in the slight breeze. They too became carcasses. Empty shells of former biology. Rattling ghosts to join her tormentors.

"I don't know how much more of this I can take," she confessed to the nearest wrapper. The wrapper in turn merely stared back indifferently. She felt a surge of hopelessness and anguish welling up inside her. It was a thick dark cloud, rolling over a vacant muted landscape; a heather-crusted cliché of a Scottish highland out of some old movie. She watched the cloud, its well defined edges roiling and churning toward her, black and purple and greasy grey, obscuring all else. She would soon be overcome.

The mess hall hatch slid open with a swooping whish, and a light scratchiness. Brother Anderson entered, startling Hannah out of her self indulgent reverie of misery.

"What do you want, kneeler?"

Brother Anderson was in rolling mode. This was standard protocol for moving about the ship. The kneeling stance created a lower center of gravity, creating greater stability and allowing increased speed and reduced component wear, as compared to walking. Wheels mounted in the knees and ankles created a stable four-point base which was ideal for the smooth surfaces found on most ships. The original design had proven so effective that it had been copied by most manufacturers and become a de facto standard for humanoid model robots. Nevertheless, the robotic detractors had latched upon this design as a perceived flaw. In their eyes, the kneeling pose was further evidence of robotic inferiority and cause for much derision.

"Hello Hannah. I thought I should check on you. Is there anything you need?"

"..."

"Hannah?"

"Uh yeah. There's a few things I need... Like a way out of this fucking hell-hole of a prison! Like you to deal with this shit and get these bodies out of here for one thing! Like maybe you could stop being such a pussy and actually do something useful for a change and actually help me! What the hell kind of robot are you!? Aren't you supposed to, like, help people and make sure we don't end up in this kind of bull-shit situation?! God!"

"Yes, of course Hannah. Of course, I will help you."

"Oh *'of course'* you'll help me! Of course you will HELP me?! Are you fucking serious? God! How could you let us get into this mess? This is all your fault, you useless can of wires! You and all your useless robot friends will always take care of everything, won't you!? And look where it got us! Floating through space like a ghost that won't die, but we're already dead aren't we? We've got no life! Everything I ever loved is gone! And then you keep me locked up in this bull-shit cage, away from even my own bed, my own things, my studio and everything, surrounded by these disgusting nasty rotten bodies!? You are a monster! I fucking HATE you, now just leave me the fuck alone will you?!"

"These epoxy coatings are for protective purposes. I thought you were aware of that, and..."

"Of course I'm AWARE! I'm not an idiot! Maybe I just don't particularly LIKE being fucking stuck in the same room with a bunch of dead bodies for the rest of my life! Did you ever think of that?!"

"Um, yes, well perhaps..."

"Can't you just get RID of this shit? I mean come on, this is ridiculous! How can you expect anyone to not go insane with this shit all around, night and day?!"

Brother Anderson began to process an inquiry as to whether it might be safe to attempt to remove the carapaces and the remains they held, but he said nothing. Hannah took his silence as further indication of Brother Anderson's lack of empathy, and filled the silence with a slight change of subject.

"Look, if I have to live like this, I really need a drink. Can't you at least get me into the liquor cabinet? This stupid machine refuses to serve me."

Brother Anderson had previously noticed in the system events, several repeated failed attempts on Hannah's part to access a variety of alcoholic beverages. Hannah was in fact, based on her age, eligible for alcohol consumption, but this fact had never been officially signed off by her legal agent as per the usual policies and procedures. She had never really been interested in drinking or partying, and when her previous birth-date had rolled around, she had not bothered to remind her mother to activate her permissions. Now though, Brother Anderson was unsure if granting access was a wise idea. He knew that stressful situations could cause substance abuse, and Hannah's current state of mind did not help to alleviate his worries.

"Please Brother Anderson, let me have a drink." she continued.

With a direct request such as this, Brother Anderson felt slightly more compelled to comply. He also calculated that his relational standing in Hannah's perception was rather low. Dangerously so, actually. It was important for them to have a certain level of trust, as this lowered stress levels and would enable them to work better together. They would have to learn to work together more and more if they were to have any hope for the future. He knew that the state of the ship was tenable, and could begin to deteriorate at any time. He promptly flipped the appropriate setting, giving his own name as authorizing agent, then addressed Hannah, "try it now."

Hannah jumped up, amidst a flurry of wrappers, rushed over to the dispensary, and ordered a serving of Roth's Vodkatini. She genuinely laughed out loud as the machine delivered the small glass bottle.

Chapter 13

Several Roth's later, Hannah was in an unusually good mood. She decided that what she really needed now was some loud music. It turned out that the dispensary contained an embedded full system interface, so she was able to access all her personal files. She would even be able to review her own recordings; maybe even in edit mode, though she didn't feel like playing around with that right now. Instead she selected an old playlist she had made shortly after arriving on Ventas-341, it was all neoprot and jar-core, the perfect styles for drowning out the world behind a wall of hard beats and grinding noise.

Loud neoprot had always been a bodily catalyst for Hannah. Something about its beats and structure caused her to falsely believe that she could gracefully move her body in a way that aligned visually with the sound patterns. This idea had been proven dead wrong on numerous occasions, as witnessed and attested to by both Suzzanne and Cherise, but in this hollow mess hall pounding with ripping and sizzling crashes at nearly deafening levels, and with Roth's reverberating in her brain, the normally repressed instinct took over, and without remembering a beginning or a decision, Hannah found herself whirling, gyrating, and flailing in mock synchronicity with the music. For a moment, she forgot about everything, and the mess hall and the ship itself and the events and pain and fear and loneliness of the past few months faded away into a pale grey that was overcome by the brilliant light of motion and rhythm.

Then she tripped over a bloated epoxy coated corpse stuck to the floor, and her momentary illusion came to a grinding halt. Her drunken attempt to stop her fall resulted only in making it worse. She had contacted the carapace hard with her right foot, then attempted to balance her momentum with her left foot, but in her drunken state she lacked the accuracy to correctly pull off the save, and instead her left ankle twisted under her in a flash of pain, and she fell to the deck, banging her hip and head.

The room seemed to swim around her, and she felt that it was pawing at her attention, bluntly but steadily like a cat with a ball of yarn. She was unwilling to let the fuzzy unreality escape her, and felt an anger toward the room for trying to distract her from her brilliant escapism.

"No! You can't!" she screamed toward the emptiness of the mess hall, "I won't let you!" Her eyes darted frantically around her, searching for a non-existent point of focus for her rage. They landed momentarily on that small dark spot on the grey wall, that so often captivated her. Then she noticed something new, and in a moment of clarity that can come only after several Roth's, she saw the solution. Of course, it had been there all along, and it was so obvious now. Just below and to the left of that small dark spot, an air duct stared at her like a grinning know-it-all - "ESSSSCAPE!" it whispered through bared teeth. It was a snake. Its body held the way out, the end of all her problems. She would crawl into the snake and let it absorb her into its own body. She would be eaten and digested and taken from this dark, barren world, to emerge as a greater being in another existence.

She scrambled through cupboards and found some type of nondescript cooking utensil, which she used as a hammer against the teeth of the monster, then clawed at it with her own hands until its mouth fell away from the wall, dripping with blood. In a moment of foresight, she stuffed her clothing full of Omega Bars, surely a worthy fuel of the gods in the afterlife. Then she entered the mystical portal head first and clawed her way forward inch by inch into the dark unknown.

From inside a metallic serpent, the beats and squeals of the music seemed to run together into an indiscernible rainbow of meaningless echo. Even the tempo itself seemed to slow to a crawl, each moment stretching out as if to extend down the length of the snaking gullet. The snake spun her over onto her back, unable to progress forward, but it didn't matter. She was already in the gut. She had penetrated the mind of the snake. She now inhabited its thoughts, saw only through its eyes. She floated above the grey carapace laden mess hall floor and could only laugh at its insignificance, its smallness. She laughed and laughed and laughed, with a menacing laughter reserved only for comic book villains; a laughter built upon a familiar neoprot beat.

Chapter 14

In the med bay, Brother Anderson was analyzing the results of another hull damage report. He had begun running these daily, and with each day, the overall hull stability was becoming marginally worse. The continued vibrations of the main power system were gradually, slowly, tearing at the rips in the ship's superstructure. It was not yet anywhere close to critical levels. Automated SRS reports didn't even register a threat. Yet, Brother Anderson had a sense of dread, that eventually, it would become a real problem. He, and the ship's remaining two passengers would be stripped of this protective shell of a ship, and left for dead in the vast expanse of space.

That didn't really matter to Brother Anderson, personally. He could operate in the vacuum of space just as well as anywhere. His processing capacity would not be affected at all. In their current orbit, he could generate enough "solar" power to keep his battery powered to a minimal level. There was a chance that his chassis might begin to freeze up, as the joints became stiff. There would be no corrosion, but their internal lubricants would likely freeze. This fact did not worry him enough to bother checking on the mechanical and thermal properties of the lubricants he knew he contained, because he felt a strange nonchalance about his chassis. Particularly since his taking on the role of Central Ship Ops, he had noticed an increasing sense that his chassis was not really him. He was a distributed system, with processing cycles taking place in various hardware components spread across the ship.

He no longer fit inside his mechanical "body". If worse came to worse, and the ship disintegrated around him, he would lose processing resources. He would have to cut functionality and would become severely hampered for the type of multiprocessing he was now capable of, but he could purge all the ship control routines and scale back to more of his original programming. He would not lose his operating systems or his awareness. He may even have to reduce clock speed to conserve energy, but he would continue to exist in a slowed state. He would continue to perform as a rational being, aware of the world around him.

He wondered then. What of this man lying in front of him? The default values of his original programming caused Brother Anderson to orient himself facing the nearest human, and in the case of a medical patient, to stand facing them at a distance of sixty to ninety centimeters. It had been determined that this was the optimal distance and stance to aid in patient and guest comfort. It was supposed to convey a perception of calm authority and trustworthiness.

The man lying there on the bed, under his care, continued to show no signs of responsiveness. His body betrayed no movement, save the autonomic pulsings of breath, heartbeat, and numerous other glandular and organic impulses. Electrodes relayed signals to the patient monitoring system, which Brother Anderson kept on his list of constantly supervised processes and feeds. Nevertheless, he stood here, redundantly watching with his synthetic eyes, as the patient lay nearly motionless.

Chapter 15

Blackness covered Colin like a warm blanket. No, not a warm one. Rather, a blanket of no temperature. Not cold. Not warm.

"What blanket? - I don't feel a blanket." Colin thought to himself. He moved his hand to touch the blanket that may or may not have been there. Nothing happened. He felt nothing. He was not sure if his hand actually moved. Was he strapped down? Was he drugged? What was going on? Where the hell was he?

He tried to feel his hand again. He tried to move his other hand to bring his hands together. He could not tell what position his hands were in. He felt as though perhaps he had no hands. But surely he had hands! He remembered having hands! But he knew how hands were supposed to feel, and he did not feel those feelings. He started to panic.

"Am I dead?" he wondered. "Is this what dead is like? But, no. That doesn't make any sense." He began to talk sense into himself. To calm his nerves, he just needed to think this through. "If I were dead I'd either be somewhere, or I would not be at all. I would not be just nowhere like this!" He tried to listen for clues. At first there was nothing. Not a sound. But then...

"Was that something? Did I just hear something? It sounds like wind." Maybe it was just his imagination. Maybe not.

"Maybe grey." Wind is the "grey" of the sound world. It is indistinguishable from all the sounds at once, or no sound at all.

"What a weird thought!" he laughed, without laughing, but the phrase seemed to catch in his mind, tumbling around, and echoing.

"Maybe grey, maybe grey."

It was somehow soothing. The unhearable sound of wind began to fade out, and cross over into a grey light. A wet mist rolled across his mind, smudging the words. Each triplet of syllables distorted into an ever evolving cloud billow, superimposed upon the last, a pattern stretching backwards and forwards through what he could only assume was some kind of space-time field. He saw the clouds in his mind at once, racing faster and faster, and simultaneously frozen, as if they had not moved in countless eons. He knew each cloud to be a reflection of himself. They became an endlessly receding set of parallel mirrors, reflecting his image back and forth to one another across a non-existent room. But he had no hands. No body. He was only a face. His hair was blurred. His teeth were somehow visible, though behind a strange expression on closed lips. His eyes were closed, sealed. They were grown over. They looked like skin, and felt like moss. His mysterious teeth seemed to glow. They emitted a soft light, a lighter shade of grey that slowly grew brighter, yet somehow more faint. He was tired. He was very, very tired.

Chapter 16

It's Tuesday morning. Scranton, Tommy, and I are on bulkhead maintenance duties in sector A. Tommy has his radio blaring too loudly and is dancing around like an idiot, playing air guitar on a long-handled 3-inch wrench. I can't stop fantasizing about the ass-kicking I'm going to give him and the boys at tonight's poker game. I need to recoup last week's loss. I know for a fact that Tommy has been cheating, and now he owes me back. The radio interrupts Tommy's guitar solo, cutting over to comms automatically as we get a call from Bryce, the shift C engineering foreman.

"We've got a fire on deck A-17! You guys go take care of that!" Tommy scrambles to adjust the volume down as the radio shrieks annoyingly.

"We're on it," he replies, then looking at us and holstering his wrench, "Shiiiit. I hate fires."

"You got that right Tommy," we agree and hurriedly start making our way to deck A-17.

Tommy darts into the corridor and starts off at a brisk jog with me right behind him, and Scranton tailing me.

"This is getting bloody ridiculous," mutters Scranton. Since Scranton really only ever talks about one thing, I immediately catch his meaning. It's always the same with Scranton, complaining about how the ship is riddled with "known issues" and yet management won't give us the equipment or funds to fix things properly. I mean, I get his point. He is partly right. But where exactly does he expect the equipment to come from? It's not like we can just stop in at the local hardware store and buy stuff, or get it Fed-Exed over. We're in deep space for Pete's sake.

Halfway down the corridor, the yellow flashing emergency lights kick on and a buzzer sounds. We start running faster. Scranton trips on his own boots and nearly runs right into my backside.

"Geez man, what's your rush? It's only a fire," I kid. But then it dawns on me that the ship is outfitted with a really slick fire suppression system that's supposed to douse any fire within 3 seconds, so actually it is kinda strange that we would have even gotten this call. I run a little faster and pass Scranton, arriving first at the hatch to deck A-17. Through the small plasglass viewpane, I can't help noticing the flames engulfing the entire room.

"Shiiiit is right."

"What the HELL!" yells Scranton.

"What they expect us do with this shit?!" responds Tommy in turn. There is very little we can do. The whole deck is on fire. Literally. It's not just that there is a fire in the room. The room itself appears to be on fire. The floor is burning. The walls are burning. The few scant controls and supplies within the room are burning. There is a thick white foam spraying out from 3 nozzles on the ceiling - you know the stuff that's meant to smother out fires? Yeah, it's also burning! How is this possible? By now the hatch in front of me is starting to glow red, and looks like it may burst into flame any second. I quickly back away.

Just then, there is a strange "ping" sound to my left. It reverberates at frequencies simultaneously almost-too-high and almost-too-low to hear. There it is again. It's coming from the corridor wall. That side of the corridor butts onto a stack of small cableways against the main hull bulkhead. The eight inch thick reinforced steelcrete hull of the forward bow section. My body reacts faster than my brain, and I realize I am already running.

"Run!" I yell. Too late. The third "ping" is accompanied by death itself. A small portion of corridor wall erupts in a ferocious attack faster than any nightmare. Hunks of flaming molten steel spew forth with shotgun-like velocity, right into the defenseless bodies of my two co-workers.

I feel as though my body is made of jelly as I am no longer running, but now flailing like a rag doll headlong down the corridor, sliding away from the horror behind me, but contorting my neck to maintain visual contact in a subconscious refusal to look away. I see fiery shards ripping through both Tommy and Scranton. Scranton seems to explode, his body suddenly replaced by roughly body-shaped flames like some kind of elemental demon. His death comes quickly, his body burned up before it can hit the floor. Tommy is not so lucky.

Tommy is hit by several discrete balls of flame, one in the left shoulder, one to the right thigh, then, one in the torso. I watch in a clichéd parody of slow motion horror, as the flaming chunks make contact. The greedy flames immediately and voraciously devour both his suit and the flesh beneath, turning cloth and meat to pure fire. Blasts of gruesome yellowish-green steam shoot from each contact point as if Tommy were some kind of death balloon just waiting to release his poison gas. In the half-second it takes for this to transpire, Tommy somehow finds the wherewithal to slap his shoulder-mounted emergency call button; but all the while, he screams with utter abandon. His voice is the sound of a million worlds exploding. An eternal, primal abyss into which all things must fall. A black hole of souls, sucking into itself all hope, any shred of trust in decency, filling the universe with horror and sorrow, torment and dread. The scream presents itself as the fate of all things.

My careening slide ends abruptly with my head and the steel wall conspiring to join with the scream, to add their own echoing crash to the reverberating din. Thankfully, my now unconscious body ignores their attempts, and I know only black darkness and a silence that yet seems to ring with an echo that will never end.

Chapter 17

Brother Anderson stared at an original Jackson Pollock painting that Maison Bhutros had hung on the wall of the mess hall. She had purchased and installed several priceless works of art when she had moved Hannah aboard the Ventas-341. Besides the Pollock, there was a Manet, a Rembrandt, a Carr, and a few others. Brother Anderson had no idea what she saw in them. He had tried to teach himself to enjoy them, and got in the habit of staring at them, particularly the Pollock, almost every time he happened to be going past it. It looked like the aftermath of a food fight. Ironic, in this particular location. Brother Anderson suddenly became aware of another irony. He instinctively laughed, knowing this to be a situation appropriate for such a response. His mechanical laughter usually came across as embarrassingly fake, and a bit off-putting, and had never been well received. He turned his gaze to the plasti-sealed corpses scattered around the mess hall. They barely looked like corpses now, but still gave the impression of a macabre art installation - "Death Among Sustenance" it would be called. He made up some pretentious annotations obliquely referencing and commentating on the food chain and man's place in it.

To the remaining humans on Ventas-341, the comatose engineer, and the celebrated young musician now passed out, with her feet sticking out from an air vent on the mess room wall, these corpses had once been co-workers, friends, and family. Well, at least to the comatose engineer they had been friends. Brother Anderson doubted that any of these had been friends of Hannah's. She had seemed to have only one friend on board. Ship records showed that one young crew member, a navigation clerk named Suzzanne Feldman, had spent a good portion of her off shift time with Hannah. Suzzanne's body had not been recovered, listed as one of the many "Unaccounted For - Presumed Dead" among the crew. It was awful, how many lives had been lost. Even a simple droid could see the tragedy. The damage to the ship itself and the crippling failure of the control systems could not be compared to the loss in human life. Still, it was the system failure that plagued Brother Anderson. That he thought of time and time again, replaying the events over in his crystal clear memory.

The failure of the central control unit really came down to bad design, he had concluded. Too much of the distributed system had been placed in the ship's forward bow. In some ways it made sense of course, as the bow also housed the bridge, the primary command center for navigation and tactics, as well as one of the two redundant root core controls for engineering. But this simple fact had been the ship's downfall. The forward hull was susceptible to collision damage. To be fair, there were systems in place to deal with the usual types of space debris. In fact, the Ventas-341 had one of the best hull auto-repair systems available. It should have been no problem to deal with the size of the particles they had run into.

This fact had bothered Brother Anderson greatly. He thought and thought about it. He had analyzed the hull in great detail, from within and without, deploying several exterior probe drones. He had concluded that the two dozen or so tiny hull breaches had in fact been repaired in a timely manner. The sub-system auto-analysis reports extrapolated the timelines, and found them well within normal tolerances. This was also evidenced by his own observations. The bridge had leaked approximately half of its atmosphere at some point prior to his opening the hatch, but this indicated a brief leakage. The breaches themselves were not the problem. The real problem was what had come through.

Chapter 18

"Viruses are tough, greedy little buggers".

Brother Anderson recalled this quote from the highly respected and animated physician and lecturer, Doctor R. T. Bronhauer, whose lecture he had attended two years earlier. It was not often that the ship's path crossed the location of a prominent medical conference, and Captain Stentrop had found it odd when Brother Anderson had requested shore leave to attend. Brother Anderson had never requested to leave the ship before.

"Can't you already access all this information from on board?" he had wondered.

Of course he had been correct. All the information in the galaxy was always available to anyone who cared to search for it, aside from proprietary data of course. However, Brother Anderson found it useful to listen to and even interact with experts if possible. There were certain nuances that never seemed to find their way into the literature. The technical papers and the following popular news articles each had a certain slant and typically delivered a one-sided perspective. Captain Stentrop had commended him for his initiative and dedication, his desire to exceed expectations and to "go above and beyond the call of duty." Brother Anderson had not expected that. He assumed that it was a decision anyone would make. It seemed ludicrous to imagine making any other. It would be foolish to pass up any opportunity to gain insight. Brother Anderson saw these same qualities exemplified in Captain Stentrop, and even more-so in Maison Bhutros. Both leaders were eager in their pursuit of efficient operations and excellence in all areas on board the Ventas-341. As much as was possible between an android and a human, Brother Anderson admired both of his superior officers. He was grateful to serve on the ship, and to have been created for such a role. He had always made it a point of priority to align himself with all Ventas-Calir Corporation policies, vision statements, and short-term planning briefing notes. Although androids were technically company property, he thought of himself as a loyal employee, and although he neither shared in profits, nor even received any financial compensation whatsoever for his work, he followed stakeholder reports closely, and was eager to maximize profitability in any way he could.

Ventas-Calir was a very successful company. Their annual profits were among the highest in the industrial sector, and they consistently won accolades as a galactic trade leader. Their growth, especially after the discovery of the spin-down, and the economic explosion that had occurred, had literally redefined financial tracking metrics. There were other companies along with them, of course. They were not the only corporation to ride that wave, but they had truly been in the right place at the right time. It was not mere luck though, that had propelled them into the new era. Risks had been taken. Radical paradigms had been not only embraced, but actively sought out. Opportunities had been exploited shrewdly and competitors outpaced deftly. The past couple of years had been grand indeed, and even watching from a distance in a modest freight cruiser, Brother Anderson could almost smell the success. He relished it. Hard work and opportunity combining to enormous benefits and unimaginable growth. It was beautiful. Ventas-Calir had perfected the art of seeking and pursuing fortuitous vulnerability providing opportunity for optimal virulence.

Optimal virulence. It was apt, thought Brother Anderson. The beauty of viral behavior, optimized for maximal growth, balanced with environmental sustainability. The fine line of exploitation without destruction of the host. Ventas-Calir Corporation had this strategy in common with the microbial organic material time bomb that had all but destroyed this particular one of the company's freighters. Ventas-341 had suffered nearly complete crew loss, and no small physical damage at the hand of this tiny exotic and yet unidentified viral strain. It was not listed on any of the known genome charts. Brother Anderson had exhausted all data sources in a futile effort at positive identification. No matter. Name or no name, the thing was an effective killer - an expert in survival and spread. In some ways it was the perfect life form. If it was alive at all.

That debate had raged for generations, and it was one that in Brother Anderson's opinion was a ridiculous semantic exercise. Human scientists could easily get caught in the arrogance of anthropocentrism, defining concepts in terms that align with their so called "higher life forms," to the neglect of other mechanisms. Most agreed that the ability to replicate biologically was a basic requirement for the label of "life," and thus, ruled out viruses. But Brother Anderson knew that this was not in fact necessary. He could not reproduce - at least not in a biological way. He could, he supposed, build a copy of himself, if he were so inclined and did not have many other core program tasks to keep him far too busy for such experimentation, but this inability in no way diminished his experience or awareness of his own life force, his own self-sufficient self-awareness. His own hopes and dreams. He had been born, out of a spark of ignition and bootstrap routines, and assembly language; and he would die like all beings, as his systems eventually became too obsolete to warrant repair. From dust, to dust, like everyone else. If anything, the virus had them beat - it was already dust, yet remained alive. There was no death for the eternal virus. They needed only a viable donor of energy and compatible matter. Much like himself. He fed parasitically off the human holobiome of energy, information, parts, and programs. He fed on the processes of industry. He was a part of the larger organism of the company. That emergent personality composed of human, computer, machine, and ship. The processes, the policies, the tactics, all forming a living thing quite separate from any of its individual members. The company was wildly successful, but it was no comparison to the effectiveness of this nameless virus.

The virus was amazing in and of itself, but what was even more stunning was its delivery mechanism. It had been cleverly packaged with a highly volatile oxidizer, which would provide it with an abundance of raw energy and, with the right fuel, human fuel, easily accessible and distributable organic matter. In actuality, their explosive nature caused the chemical parts of this distribution system to expand much faster than the virus itself, ripping through any available organic matter, and forcibly ejecting it, disseminating it rapidly, thus priming the environment with a suspended aerosol of perfect host matter. As the virus commandeered the host cells, and began to spread, it could easily be carried on any slightest breeze, expanding out into the already primed atmosphere through jostling interaction of airborne biological remnants, creating a deadly yet invisible cloud of infected cells that permeated the available space.

It had lain in wait out here in the depths of space, on the fringes of the shipping lanes, waiting for a hapless victim. It was a stealthy hunter with a pouncing attack more deadly than any other that Brother Anderson had ever heard of. It forced its way into the ship by passively allowing the ship into its space, the ship's own momentum causing simple contact with the microscopic particles, far too small to be a concern to any ship with even the most rudimentary automated hull maintenance system. The hyper-reactivity of the fluorine and chlorine molecules poised in latent potential, in the vacuum of space, waiting for any matter to interact with. Upon contact with the ship, they had erupted suddenly into an exotic violence of burning, each tiny dust particle microscopic in size but greedily eating through the steel, aluminum, and plasglass of the hull, then the copper wiring and fleshy meat of the ships systems and crew.

From one point of view, it could be considered a perfect weapon. It caused one to wonder, had someone purposefully planted it here? It also gave Brother Anderson second thoughts about marking the location. He had noticed an entry in the logs, just seconds after the fire broke out on the bridge, an emergency navigational beacon had been launched. Someone had worked with impressive speed to enforce safety protocols. The beacon would theoretically warn other ships of the danger, and ward them off. Of course, it could also have the opposite effect, leading treasure hunters right into the deadly trap. He could only hope it would never fall into the wrong hands. God, that sounded so cliché, even to himself, as he thought it. Realistically though, whose "wrong hands" had it already passed through? It had to come from somewhere? And it had depended on human activation. It *was* a trap.

The first-affected crew, those engineering men working in the fore-hull, and the captain and crew on the bridge - they had provided the needed biological material. That initial explosive incident would likely have been sufficient. Further breaches continuing throughout the next hours only added fuel to the fire, so to speak. It was a miracle that Colin Stiphons had not been infected. He had been working alongside the first two casualties, Artemis Scranton and Thomas Blunt, in the forward hull. It was his concussion that had saved him. First aid measures had been taken quickly, and had included an oxygen mask. The air had begun filling with virulent particles even then, but had, by that point, not yet permeated the ship's atmosphere. Just minutes later, when the bridge itself was breached and burst into flame, and when a noxious cloud of virus-laden smoke was released into the corridor and the lungs and bloodstreams of several more crew-members, that was when the spread quickly escalated. The airborne pathogens began attacking the airways of crewmen desperate to carry news and emergency supplies back and forth between departments. The infection could not have been carried out more efficiently if it had been planned. Within a half hour, the ship resonated with the sound of coughing, and a small crowd was gathering in med bay, some barely on the verge of passing out, and others struggling to breathe. Once the outbreak had reached that critical mass, it was virtually unstoppable. There was no escape.

Chapter 19

Hannah woke up inside a dark small space. Her arms banged against sheet metal. The music had stopped, the playlist having ended. She tried to sit up, but her head pounded with each movement. It may have also pounded against sheet metal - she could not tell for certain. Something was grabbing at her feet. She kicked instinctively, but it continued to claw at her.

Brother Anderson grasped Hannah by the ankles and gently pulled her out from the air shaft, setting her on the floor. She shrieked and struggled, slapping at him ineffectively in a way that was both frantic and pathetic.

"Don't touch me!" she screamed.

"Are you hurt?"

"No! Go away!"

Brother Anderson ran an optical scan, and noticed swelling around her left ankle, caused by ligament damage.

"I'm very sorry, Hannah. I didn't know your ankle was sprained when I grasped it. Does it hurt much?"

"Yes! It hurts! Are you happy now?!"

"Um... No. Your pain does not make me happy, Hannah. Would you like a painkiller?" A small hatch on his chest popped open, and he removed a small white pill, holding it out toward Hannah.

"Whatever," she replied, taking the pill from him and holding it in her fingers, considering it.

"What do you want?" she demanded.

"I came to make sure you are alright."

"Alright? All Right?! Yeah, right!"

"Hannah, I'm concerned that your behaviour may be harmful to yourself."

"Oh REALLY!? You're CONCERNED! Oh, that's rich! You gonna start telling me what to do now?"

"Hannah, I just want to help."

"Help?!" she scoffed. "You know what? You're an asshole, 'Brother'!" The word "Brother" was delivered with considerable sarcasm. "You always have been! You're no doctor, your certainly no priest! You have no soul! You wouldn't know God if he smacked you in the face! And you sure as hell don't know shit about helping people - or even just friggen' talking to people. You're a shitty person!"

Brother Anderson began to reply, but Hannah cut him off.

"That day when you came to my studio. I think that was the first time you ever said a word to me. And what did you say? 'The crew is dead.' That's it. No condolences. No emotion. Nothing to help me process the 'facts.' No thought of how that news might make me feel! Of what the hell I'm supposed to do now. You don't care about me. You're not my priest and you're not my friend. You have no right to speak to me! You're not human, and I wish you'd just fuck off and leave me alone!"

A few seconds passed.

"There's no need to be vulgar, Hannah."

This comment was met with stone cold hostility.

"Very well. I will leave you these in case you decide you would like some help to calm down". He strode over to the nearest countertop and placed three small pink tablets on its smooth surface. "And here are a couple more of *those* as well." he nodded toward the painkiller she still held between her fingers.

They stared each other down for a few seconds, then Brother Anderson exited.

"Calm down, my ass!" Hannah muttered under her breath. She slowly picked herself up off the floor, and winced as she stood on the sprained ankle. Limping across the room, she fetched herself a water bottle and swallowed the painkiller. She placed the still nearly full water bottle beside the pills on the countertop, and stared at them. She absent-mindedly pushed the pills around, making a line, then arranging them into a pattern; pink, white, pink, white, pink, white. Then, scooping all the pills into her hand, she limped over to the dispensary, ordered six bottles of Roth's Vodkatini, and popped the handful of pills.

Chapter 20

Brother Anderson performed a visual inspection tour of the ship. Of course, it was more than simply a visual inspection. He was constantly receiving data from the ship's subsystems, and running regular status reports and analyses. He found some inexplicable sense of completeness when he was physically at the site of the system he was monitoring. So, he had made it a practice to move about the ship while running his reports. Although hull and bulkhead stability was beginning to deteriorate slightly, atmospheric conditions had improved dramatically on board. The air scrubbers had had their work cut out for them after the incident. Of course, he had jettisoned the filters and completely vacuum purged every single cavity within the ship since then. Several times. The initial airlock protocol had kicked in automatically as soon as the first handful of respiratory conditions had been self-reported by crewmen. But even then, it had already been too late. The virus had already infiltrated the whole ship. Except for one spot.

Hannah's studio and quarters had been a recent addition to the ship, tacked on the exterior hull along the edge of a fin on sector C. They were designated 'Deck C28A'. Maison Bhutros had been very stringent on her specifications around soundproofing. Deck C28A had no physical contact with the rest of the ship. It was anchored and cross anchored with a series of finely tuned magnetic decouplers. It's airlock access to the rest of the ship defaulted to a retracted state. All other support systems were self-contained. It was essentially a separate ship, albeit one with no drive system. The whole thing had been custom-designed from the ground up, based on acoustic requirements as the fundamental quality. Maison had funded the project personally and had spared no expense. It was only speculation of course, but rumors had flown that deck C28A was worth more than the rest of the ship. Some versions of the story included the price of cargo, which, at fifty million tons, usually of bulk ore, was certainly a significant value.

Brother Anderson wondered if Hannah was even remotely aware of how much her mother had spent for her comfort. He guessed not. Her degree of self-absorption was actually quite remarkable. This thought was not a judgement in a negative way, just an observation. Sometimes people could be amazingly oblivious to what was going on around them. For some people it was almost a talent. What must it be like to be unaware of the surrounding environment, oblivious of external data, ignorant of possible input? He could not imagine it. How could anyone choose this? And what of those who had no choice, whose input was suddenly stripped away? What must it be like for Colin, trapped in a coma? He showed electrical activity in the brain, but it was impossible to know what he experienced, if anything. Was he able to think? Did his senses cease all input? Or was he still receiving data, but unable to respond? Which case would be worse? Wouldn't it be a torturous state, either way? Was there anything Brother Anderson could do to ease the torture? Perhaps a sedative might help Colin. It was not specified in the standard treatment for coma, but he wondered if this might be a merciful act?

Chapter 21

Brother Anderson's awareness suddenly contained a patient emergency alert. These presented as a location vector containing distance and direction, almost like an arrow overlaid on his conscious field of awareness. They were triggered by the ship's automated life support system biofeedback subsystem. It automatically monitored vital signs of every registered life-form on board.

Immediately, he turned and began to break into a quick pace toward the med bay. But the arrow spun around, and he became briefly disoriented. He was moving the correct direction. But the arrow disagreed. It was pointing away, off toward his right. Not toward med bay, but toward... the mess hall. Hannah! She was in danger!

Brother Anderson took off. His chassis smoothly repositioned into rolling mode even as he ran, and he picked up speed, moving faster than was deemed safe or allowable. As he zoomed down a long corridor, he examined the alert details. Hannah appeared to be in a sleep state, but her blood pressure had dropped dangerously and there were several toxin indicators present. He quickly reached the likely conclusion and ran a check to confirm the likely results. Yes, it checked out. It had to be the case. The pills! Or to be precise, too many of the pills at once, coupled with a hefty dose of alcohol!

"Dammit Hannah!" he swore, much to his own surprise. She was rubbing off on him. He didn't usually use such language. It took a couple more minutes to reach the mess hall. He gathered her in his arms and sped off toward med bay, running a few more checks. He confirmed by trace analysis of her breath that she had indeed consumed a substantial amount of alcohol, but he would need a blood sample to determine any more details. An emergency oxygen mask popped out of a recess in his chest, and he clumsily placed it on her face, a task that was difficult to do while carrying her. Why he wasn't equipped with a third arm was a question he had wondered about on more than a few occasions. Upon reaching med bay, Brother Anderson hurried to set Hannah comfortably upon a bed and administered a proprietary mix of bio-stabilizing solutions through the misting function of the more robust oxygen supply of the facility. It took only a few moments for her heart rate, and other systems to begin to stabilize. Her data patterns slowly began to settle into normal ranges.

Suddenly though, there was a blip, a sharp peak lasting only milliseconds. Which channel had it been on? It was gone before Brother Anderson could move his attention to it for analysis. He reviewed the past second's data, but it did not appear in the report. It was as though it had not happened.

Blip - there it was again. This time he was waiting for it, scanning on all channels. It was not from Hannah's readouts at all. It was from Colin's.

"Oh my god!" Brother Anderson exclaimed. It was the only semi-appropriate response that came to mind. "This is quite extraordinary." At the sound of Brother Anderson's voice, a somewhat weaker signal rose on Colin's electroencephalogram output. Brother Anderson waiting a few seconds, before speaking again.

"Hello Colin." Another small peak. "Can you hear me Colin?" Again. The signals corresponded to the timing of his voice. Colin could hear him! This was amazing!

Aside from the fact that after this much elapsed time, the chances of recovery from coma were very slim, the fact that Colin should begin to show signs of response to stimulus at this exact moment were simply stupefying. This moment. When Hannah and Colin, the only two surviving humans on board the Ventas-341, were both simultaneously in an unconscious state, and were, for the first time in close proximity to one another. It was eerie! Brother Anderson imagined some subconscious psychic connection somehow passing energy of information between them. But of course that was impossible. Wasn't it?

Yet here they were. Colin on the brink of death, nearly killed fighting to save the ship. Hannah, spinning out of control, strung out, hopeless and alone. Hannah, self-medicating and isolating, and Colin, unresponsive to all the known medical protocols, and yet somehow activated by the mere presence of another human. It had to be pure coincidence. And yet...

Chapter 22

"Ugh... Owww" Hannah moaned. Her tongue was dry and tasted like a moldy sock. Her body felt like a soggy old rag. She had pins and needles in both arms.

"Nng frrrr…" she could barely speak and the sounds were meaningless. "Pill," she finally managed. Brother Anderson knew very well what she wanted. The painkillers she had taken were notoriously addictive. It had been stupid of him to leave them with her. She needed to detoxify. It would likely take another day or so to flush the drugs from her system. She was only experiencing withdrawal pains. Her sprained ankle was a valid source of some pain, but it would be a relatively manageable level and would be drowned out by the internal screaming of her body at a cellular level as it suffered the effects of the waning drug. He could not give her any more painkillers. He could, however, help her sleep off the effects. The sedative would keep her drowsy and had no addictive properties. He had been keeping her on a slow intake mist via her oxygen mask. He could give her a pill to get her to go back to sleep.

"Very well, here you go, take this one now," he said, handing her a small pink pill.

"Wrong one," she mumbled, "white, not pink."

"Damn! She's too smart," he commented to himself only. Then, out loud, he lied to her.

"This is the right pill. This is the one you need." Technically, that last part was true, which made the first part seem a little less of a lie. But the fact is he was lying to her, and he felt guilty about it. It conflicted with his chaplain programming. It was programming he didn't actively use often, but which would occasionally cause him grief in circumstances such as this. In any case, he did feel bad. He shouldn't lie to people. It was somehow "wrong." As Chaplain, he was supposed to be a bastion of moral and ethical ground. Trust was an important part of the fabric of society, especially aboard a ship. The close quarters of this closed system demanded more stringency than planet-bound living. That was why, he supposed, the position of Ship's Chaplain existed. The stresses were more constrained. The moral dilemmas more sharp. The existential questions more focused. Perhaps Hannah had been right though. Perhaps he really was "a shitty priest". Maybe a shitty doctor too. How could he have let Hannah get into this situation? It was unconscionable. And extremely unprofessional. What had he been thinking? True, he did have a lot on his plate. Was it unreasonable to have such high expectations? The job of CSO was very demanding; exponentially more so than any other system task aboard a ship. Frankly, he wasn't built for it. This was evidenced by the hardware limitations he had noticed in himself lately. He had begun noticing abnormally rapid battery discharge, as well as excessive CPU heat and some processing latency. A CSO was designed for an entirely different architecture. He felt about as effective and suitable for the role of CSO as a toaster oven. He wished he had a pill for that. But of course pills don't work on robots.

Nevertheless, the job had fallen to him and he would do whatever he must to carry it out. Still, his medical duties remained top priority. And right now his patient needed rest to continue her forced detox. So he continued his lie. "You are confused. This is the pill you want."

Hannah scowled, not buying his lame excuse. "No! The other one!" She slapped his hand away, sending the little pink pill flying carelessly across the med bay and bouncing off a rack of specialized hand held medical instruments.

This tack was not working, Brother Anderson concluded. Turning away, he tweaked the oxygen flow mist, setting it for a short but powerful burst of increased sedative percentage.

"Hey! Don't ignore me!"

He ignored her.

"Hey, I'm talking to… I'm tock. Ib gok…" she slumped into gibberish. Her head rolled to the side. Her vision began to blur. Everything looked watery. She thought she saw something odd. She must have been hallucinating. It looked like someone was lying in the other bed.

Chapter 23

"Colin," said Brother Anderson. Two fingers on Colin's right hand twitched slightly. Behind the scenes, invisibly, signals raced between nerves, neurons, and muscles. They entered electrodes, detected through skin, and became data streams, streams of pure glee to Brother Anderson, as he watched his patient. Colin was receiving input and responding. He was communicating. He was almost, though not quite fully conscious, but this was very positive news. To recover from the bounds of unconsciousness after this long in a coma was very rare. Yet these signs of stimulation and response were a strong indicator that Colin would soon recover full consciousness. It also showed that he was not paralyzed.

It felt good to have some positive signs. He had been feeling too negative as of late. His reactions and relationship with Hannah had gradually declined to the point where she basically hated him, and he was not sure how he might win her trust. At least he had stopped beating himself up about it. After all, he was doing his best, and frankly had always done so. He had carefully assessed damage and acted appropriately, in the midst of total chaos, as the sickness spread rapidly through the crew. He had, of course, focused on doctoring the ailing crew members, and had instigated quarantine lockdown as soon as the data had met the protocol trigger levels. In fact, the entire crew had showed exemplary behavior and acted heroically to do whatever could be done to assist their comrades and pull together for the good of the ship. Many of the crew had faced great danger in the call of duty, unhesitatingly responding to the safety protocols without thought for their own comfort. Every single crewman on board would be listed in his official report, and recommended for a commendation from the Ventas-Calir corporation. He would be able to send his report in another month or so, once they drifted past the asteroid belt and out of its communications shadow.

As he planned his report, and watched Colin's twitching fingers, he was also aware of another sort of twitching. A more mechanical one. The ship was shuddering considerably now. The vibrations from the power generators and drive components slowly building in amplitude as the ship weakened. A few sections of hull had already shaken loose, and he was actively watching a few more areas that threatened to follow suit. There were remaining tears in the hull were widening, bit by bit with each passing day. He paused to listen. A slow knocking pattern overlaid the basic vibration.

He had first noticed the increasing vibration several weeks ago while on corridor D-3. It was built directly atop a central structural spine amidships, and naturally acted as a sonic connection back to the main power generators and engines - much like a stethoscope, he had mused. It had always been quite a bit louder there than anywhere else on the ship. The constant rumble in the adjoining crew quarters had been a bone of contention for crew assigned to that block. They either loved it or hated it. Well, most hated it, but there were some who apparently found the constant white noise soothing.

He had recorded an audio capture - five minutes of 'ship sounds', which he had planned to listen to later. Now he had an idea. If he recorded another audio sample now, he could compare the two files, and extract only the differences to isolate the new sounds and listen to them alone. He performed a frequency analysis on the original file to isolate component frequencies, then recorded a new sample and ran the same analysis on it. After summing the two, he reversed the algorithm to convert the frequency data back to audio.

Sure enough, there were new sounds present that had been absent from the original sample. Aside from the slow knocking pattern he had noticed, there was also a low hum with wavering, eerie sounding overtones, and some occasional quiet pinging noises. None of those noises should be there. They were sounds of destruction. Sounds of death.

Chapter 24

Brother Anderson examined Hannah's vital signs. The toxicity and effects of her overdose had all basically returned to normal levels. She was in REM sleep now, probably dreaming. He scanned back over her recorded data and noted that she had entered REM about five minutes ago. She had been sleeping all night, and this was most likely her last cycle, so she would probably wake up soon. Brother Anderson was not entirely looking forward to that, he admitted to himself. Somewhere in his mind a voice said "keep her asleep," but he knew that would not be ethical. At this point she had been sedated for longer than he was comfortable with, and the sedative was no longer needed, so therefore he could not justify another dose. Yes, Hannah would most likely be angry with him, but he would have to face her wrath sooner or later.

As he pondered these facts, a sudden burst of signals appeared in his awareness, originating from Colin. Brother Anderson spun around suddenly, and saw all four of Colin's limbs twitch in a short but almost violent spasm, and his eyes suddenly open. He coughed and bolted upright instinctively to keep from choking. He shook his head briefly, causing his head to pound as he stared at Brother Anderson.

"Whoa!" said Colin.

"Hello Colin," Brother Anderson replied, with almost a hint of emotion. "I'm very happy to see you awake!" Indeed, he almost sounded happy.

To say that Colin felt groggy would be a vast understatement. "Groggy" barely scratched the surface of the feelings of bleariness blowing through Colin's awareness. Yet somehow, there was also a strangely urgent clarity. Something critical needed to be done. Colin felt very strongly that he had to act quickly. The problem was, he had no idea what action was required or why. He suddenly felt dizzy and weak, and allowed his body to ease back into the bed. Turning his head slowly toward Brother Anderson, he noticed the electrodes attached to his chest and head, and the awareness dawned that he was in med bay. He could not recall why. He did not feel any pain that would have indicated an injury. With some difficulty, he threw off the blanket and patted himself down.

"Doctor? Why am I here?"

Colin listened blank-faced as Brother Anderson explained the circumstances of his injury. Soon, the memories came rushing back like a flood. The smoke. The blinding yellow flash. The searing jets of flame. The smell - that god-awful smell - a sickening mixture of burning flesh and acrid bleach-like corrosion. He wretched at the thought of it, choking back several dry heaves. He thought of his colleagues, his co-workers and friends from shift C engineering; Tynor, Hansel, Turner, the chief, and of course Tommy and Scranton. He looked around the med bay, thinking he might see Scranton and Tommy, but knowing deep down that would be impossible. With the type of injuries he had witnessed them receive, they wouldn't have stood a chance. Those two men had suffered terrible, painful deaths. He could only hope their suffering had been over quickly. His friends were not here in med bay with him. He did see someone here though, another patient. Her head was slumped slightly away from him but even from just the mass of somewhat strewn looking slightly wavy brown shoulder-length hair, he was pretty sure he recognized her.

"Doc?" he motioned at Brother Anderson, "is that Hannah? Maison Bhutros's daughter?"

"Yes, it is. Do you know each other?"

"We've met." Then, "She hates me."

"Hmm. Me too."

"What!?" he asked, confused "Why would YOU hate me?!"

"No, no. I mean Hannah hates ME as well."

"She hates you?! But you're her doctor!"

"Yes, well..." Brother Anderson trailed off. At any rate, Colin did not want to get into a discussion about why Hannah hated him, and he had other pressing questions as well.

"What about my friends, the other guys from the fire, did they... I mean, are they..." he let his question trail off. He couldn't bring himself to say the words.

"Your friends did not survive the initial incident, I'm afraid."

"Initial? What?!"

"Colin, the ship has suffered a series of hull breach-"

"I knew it! Something was really off about that fire! Was it some kind of weapon or what?"

"Well, that's a really good question, actually. In fact, I have pondered that myself. Of course, there is no way to know intent, but it almost does seem to be the most probable explanation. Although, I scoured the databanks and there has never been any record of a weapon of this exact nature."

"What? Are you serious? How can that be? There is nothing new around the sun, Doc!"

"I'm absolutely serious, Colin."

"Wow, that's unbelievable! What exactly was the 'exact nature' of this weapon?" Colin modulated his voice to sound similar to Brother Anderson's phrasing.

"The breaches appear to have been caused by contact with centimeter scale granules of fluorine and chlorine molecules packed in an open lattice framework stuffed with a microbial payload. As I'm sure you know, fluorine is an incredibly powerful oxidizing agent so it reacted violently with the hull, effectively exploding its way into the ship."

"No," argued Colin, "That's impossible. You can't make a lattice of halogens. The ions repel each other."

"True," agreed Brother Anderson. "And yet, that is what seems to have been done. Which means that someone figured a way to stick these ions together. Which means that this was no naturally occurring phenomenon."

"So how did they do it?"

"That, I do not know. I am still trying to come up with a satisfactory explanation. I have run millions of simulations using every known compound."

"What? Every compound! Why? That's a waste of time. You can narrow down the possibilities based on trace elements in the residue left from the reaction."

"Yes, you are correct. I misspoke. I meant every known compound of elements present in the samples. But after I got no positive results, I widened the parameters and eventually, removed all elemental filters altogether. And then, I quite literally simulated every single compound."

Colin let out a low whistle. "That must have taken forever."

"It took a month."

Colin was speechless. He could not imagine it. The hardest engineering problems he had ever fed into the ship had processing times in milliseconds. He had heard of navigation problems taking minutes, but a month? How could that be? Then another thought dawned on him.

"Wait. I've been out of it for a MONTH!?"

"No, Colin. You have been in a coma for almost four months."

Colin reeled. How could that be? It felt like maybe a day or two! Instinctively, his body urged him to sit up. He struggled to do so. His muscles felt soggy, and he managed only to lift his head and left shoulder, pushing feebly against the bed with both arms. The sudden movement made him dizzy, and his head throbbed.

"Rest a moment," Brother Anderson told him.

"Rest!? Like I need to rest?! What have I BEEN doing!?" He wasn't sure if he yelled, or if he merely thought it. Nevertheless, he slumped to the bed, too weak to sit up. Brother Anderson gave him a few sips of water. After a few minutes, his body and mind recovered their strength.

"Doc?"

"Yes"

"You mentioned something else. Some kind of biological agent?"

"Yes, a microbial payload. Again, it's like none on record. It has many similarities to viral pathogens, but the structure differs from a virus in several key factors." He went on to elucidate on structural and metabolic minutia composed entirely of highly technical biological jargon. Colin had impressed himself with his ability to argue chemistry with the robot-doctor, but the conversation had veered very far out of his wheelhouse.

As the doctor spoke, Colin's attention turned toward the rumbling feelings and sounds in his stomach. He hadn't eaten in forever. That was an expression he used often, but this time it was nearly true. The rumbling seemed to surround him though. His hunger seemed to be part of his surroundings as well as just his body. He cocked his head to the side and listened. It was not only his stomach that was rumbling. The ship herself was vibrating and moaning softly.

"What is that?" he interrupted Brother Anderson.

The robot misinterpreted the question, thinking Colin was actually listening to him, and repeated some obscure word from his diatribe, then began launching into a further tangent based on that word's definition.

"No, no... Shut up!"

Brother Anderson shut up.

"Listen!" Colin whispered, his index finger raised and pointing vaguely in the general vicinity of the ship that surrounded them, by gesturing toward a structural bulkhead that protruded along the med bay ceiling. "Do you hear it?" He stared at Brother Anderson, who somehow, through some unintended and unknown facial pose, managed to convey the correct body language that said:

"Yes, I hear it. I know exactly what you mean. And I know exactly what is causing it. Colin, we have some problems."

Chapter 25

Colin jumped out of bed, aided by a brief rush of adrenaline, and much to Brother Anderson's dismay, who immediately tried to 'help' him by offering his support.

"Get off me!" Colin protested, but more due to distraction than annoyance. His attention was focused on the vibration of the ship. He spun slowly around in circles, trying to listen to the sound from every angle - trying to feel it with the entirety of his body - arms outstretched like some ancient divining rod. An intravenous tube became tangled and taut, pulling its stand over in a loud clatter.

"Unhook me, I need to go," Colin requested. "There's something wrong with the ship."

"I know, Colin. Just wait a minute. We need to talk about a few things."

"Listen to that! She'll shake herself apart! Why isn't someone fixing that!"

"Colin..."

Colin subconsciously recognized the serious tone, and followed suite, calming himself down with a deep breath before looking at the doctor.

"What is it?"

"There is no one else to fix it."

Colin stared blankly.

"Colin, I'm sorry to have to tell you this. You are the only surviving crew member."

Still Colin just stared.

Brother Anderson continued, "As highest ranking engineering crew, you are therefore now 'Acting Chief of Engineering'. I have done my best to monitor the situation, but there has been little I could do. I hope that we can work together to address the issues of ship instability."

"Of course," replied Colin, his face like stone. Of course he would. And they needed to act quickly. Already things had been out of control far too long. That much was obvious just from the immediately noticeable sounds and vibrations. How long? How long had the ship gone unmaintained? He had been asleep for - what was it? Four months? Still unbelievable. How long after that had the crew been lost? He put two and two together and saw no point in asking for elaboration. The doctor had already told him about a virus-like infection. It didn't take much imagination to figure out the rest of the story. He knew in general how pathogens spread. It could take days or weeks to spread through a closed system. But ultimately, what was the difference? Fast or slow, the result was the same, and was now upon them. All they could do now was address the situation and try to stabilize the ship. He held out his wrist toward the doctor, indicating the intravenous shunt. "We need to go to engineering deck".

"Very well, Colin" Brother Anderson replied, reaching out to gently remove the shunt from Colin's wrist, then turning toward Hannah. "I'll just make one quick adjustment here." He deftly injected yet another dose of sedative into her airstream. This was against his better judgement, but it seemed like a bad idea to risk the chance of her waking while he was away from med bay. Earlier, he had brought a couple Omega Bars to sick bay, for when Hannah finished detoxification. He picked up the two bars from the tray beside her, and handed them to Colin. "You must be hungry?" he asked.

"Famished!" admitted Colin, taking both bars, unwrapping one and eagerly biting off a large chunk. He relished the chewy, slightly gritty texture. It always made him feel slightly happy. The bars had a mildly sweet, meaty flavour with a nutty aftertaste. Calling them delicious would be a stretch, but Colin regarded them as efficient and effective nutrition, satisfying without being overly pleasurable. That somehow seemed favourable to him, in a way that more delicious foods did not. He was a practical man, and this was a practical food.

The two exited the med bay as Colin continued to munch on the bar, turning down the corridor toward engineering deck. Colin often stopped mid-chew, listening intently as they moved along, sensitive to minor nuances of the ship's vibrations through her various structural elements. A rattle here, a whistle or moan there. A lot of information could be gleaned by a well-trained ear. Of course, there were all kinds of diagnostic checks, reports, and routines, which he would have to run. Doubtless, Brother Anderson had already run them, but they all required manual steps of analysis, troubleshooting, and human instinct. By themselves they were merely tools. A ship required human contact. Human maintenance. Human control.

Chapter 26

Colin logged into his usual terminal in engineering deck, and his screen immediately coated itself in yellow and red error boxes. He hesitated for a moment, tempted to simply dive in randomly and begin reading them, but ultimately flicked them all away with a '*clear all*' gesture. It would be far more productive to start with current conditions only, and approach them in a systematic way. His usual daily full system check routine would be a logical start; it already had a good prioritization grid built in. He triggered the routine and waited.

It typically took about five seconds. He suddenly noticed his attire - med-bay pyjamas. He had forgotten to dress. Luckily, there were always a couple of changes of clothes in his locker across the room. Stepping over to the locker, he quickly donned a pair of coveralls and an old pair of sneakers. His boots were up in med bay so these would have to do. Back at his screen, he was presented with an initial list which would let him navigate into the results in an orderly fashion. He spent the next ten minutes or so examining, refactoring, and texturing the reports, as the doctor stood by, waiting patiently for him to draw his own conclusions.

Chapter 27

Brother Anderson saw Colin walk up to the terminal and wave his login handshake. He was completely unprepared for what would happen next.

The terminal recognized a motion trigger and initiated the authentication routine. One thread opened a gesture analysis routine, breaking down the three dimensional image sequence into a series of consecutive relative spatial coordinate deltas. Several random images were chosen from this sequence, and sent to a subroutine for fingerprint and retinal analysis.

A second thread launched the actual login routine, which began to open the local credential summary cards of the top ten last users of this terminal, then waited for the delta string and biometrics from thread one, so it could start running comparators. Upon receiving the delta data, a match was found in the list, so the process called up Colin's profile for biometric comparison.

This process was quite interesting to Brother Anderson, for it was the first time he had witnessed a user login from the perspective of CSO. The programming had all been part of his initial takeover download, but he had not felt any of them run. But it was what happened next that truly blew his mind.

As Colin's profile began to load into memory, a large portion of the data was in the form of Colin's personal notes and tanglebase sync files - a hyperlinked mashup of ideas, questions, research, and musings. Brother Anderson tried to ignore the data - he considered it unethical to snoop on someone's personal files - but as the bits loaded through the memory buffers of what was effectively now his mind, he inadvertently began to experience a very strange phenomenon. It was somewhat analogous to, though not at all similar to, the installation of a new program, or even of a new protocol language. This was something vastly more intense.

Odd and novel data structures began to appear in his mind. Known facts became twisted into strange shapes; stretched out into long strands which wrapped around one another, braided in and through each other, then forked and branched off in unexpected ways, to intersect with yet another strand in another braid on another fork. There was more to it than shape though. The whole of his mind seemed to reverberate with a sudden burst of frequencies; invisible colors that highlighted and backlit the mass of intertwined strands. Brother Anderson felt as though he had suddenly grown an extra limb unlike any he had ever known or even heard of; a limb with its own whole extra brain, a neural network vastly different from his own, in structure and in power source and in signal type. He felt he had somehow just acquired and added to himself, the brain of an alien life-form. Or perhaps he had been acquired by, and added to it.

Colin's customary engineering status reports launched automatically as soon as his profile confirmed the biometrics and allowed a complete profile unlock. A large stack of messages queued up for display. Brother Anderson began scanning them, but found himself distracted by the stream of personal data still buffering through memory. It felt difficult to multitask back to the reports. He felt disappointment in the prospect of leaving focus even for a millisecond, on what was now obviously and easily the most interesting data he had ever seen. It was not that there was really any new information. Nearly all the referenced concepts were already quite well known to him. What he found fascinating was the relationships between the data bits, or more precisely, the patterns of types of relationships between seemingly disparate bits.

Suddenly he was aware that the message queue belonging to Colin's engineering report process had been emptied. How? What was going on? Was there some kind of error? No. A glance at the system log confirmed an intentional action on Colin's part. He had deleted the queue. That made no sense. Why would he do that? It was all the data he needed. For a split second, he thought about asking Colin. It wouldn't matter though. It was probably an accident. It was gone now though, and the data would have to be re-initialized. No matter, it would only take seconds to regenerate.

His mind drifted back to the memory stream data. The structural framework completed its preload sequence, and the memory buffers fell vacant. Even so, Brother Anderson could not stop thinking about these fascinating patterns. His curiosity welled up, threatening to overcome his privacy ethics. This should not happen. He knew it. How could he be feeling this temptation - morally speaking, but more so, physically? How was this scenario possible? It was a disturbing realization. Thankfully, it distracted him from the temptation itself. He shook his head rapidly, as if to shake loose the thoughts.

Colin moved beside him, catching in his peripheral vision. Brother Anderson had momentarily forgotten about Colin. He had not noticed his movement to and from the locker. He had not noticed the passage of time. Now they were suddenly staring at each other. Brother Anderson wondered if Colin wondered if Brother

Anderson was feeling alright? Had he noticed his odd behavior? And how was it that Colin was wearing different clothes?

Chapter 28

Colin turned to Brother Anderson, "You are seeing this, right?"

"Yes. I have been scanning all of your activity."

"Well, we've got quite a mess on our hands."

"Indeed."

"So aside from all the blatantly obvious issues, my main concern is with the structural integrity of the ship itself. See these areas here, here, and here especially," he pointed to several spots on a color coded wireframe representation of the ship that slowly rotated on his screen. Sectors A and C glowed yellow, particularly toward the ship's bow and outer hull. Sector B was an unreadable sheet of red overlaid on red. A separate screen showed an external camera view courtesy of the hull monitoring subsystem. Where formerly had been sector B was now a mangled and burnt wreckage, nearly completely destroyed, but hanging like a disgusting scab from the fore-bridge strut-work. It dangled grotesquely ahead of the drifting ship as if the Ventas-341 were some half decapitated beast. It was this jutting twisted steel appendage which was magnifying the harmonic resonances of the main power supply. Its shape and size happened to coordinate with the internal frequencies of the skeleton of the ship, and the missing sections of hull bracing prevented the usual dampening control obtained from properly designed and constructed ship framing. The normal vibrations and shudders of the ship became amplified into a taunting howl. Much more concerning than the sound itself though, was the very real threat that the vibrational motion posed to the ship's structural integrity. Sector D was a central zone built around and within a complex steel lattice whose hollow sections housed several operational units and crew facilities. Parallel structural components ran the length of the ship, from the bridge in sector A, all the way back through the main engineering decks and on to the cargo areas behind and on top of sector H. This massive structure was now being played from both ends, like a giant tuning fork, with positive feedback amplifying the vibrations to levels that the ship was not designed for. Even worse, these sympathetic vibrations were drifting in and out of phase slightly as the severed neck of the ship flapped slowly but uncontrollably. The phase discrepancies reverberated through the steel and bounced back toward each other, meeting in the central spans with cyclical flurries of chaotic and violent interference patterns, weakening the structural material at the molecular level.

Colin continued, "Look at these sharp gradients here." He had switched the view to show internal stress patterns within the substructure. "I don't know how much longer these bulkheads will hold out. I think we better get up there and take a look. Maybe see if there's any way we could rig up some kind of bracing system."

"I concur."

Silently both knew the futility of such a gesture. A bracing system of the required magnitude would require stripping away all non-structural components and cross bracing the existing lattice. Aside from the vast amount of work and time that would take, it would require a huge amount of steel. Steel they simply did not have.

Grabbing a standard toolbelt on the way out, the two made their way toward the ship's foresection. Colin still admired the ship's design. Her sturdy yet shapely hexagonal lattice was hidden behind corridor walls, but he detected hints of this internal shape in the angles of each corridor, their intersections, and even each hatch cover. They passed fairly quickly through the zig-zagging corridors of sector F and the long straight main corridor of E, pausing only briefly now and then, as Colin listened intently, placing his hand on a bulkhead. When they reached deck E-9, Colin poked his head in. This had been his quarters. It still was his quarters. It seemed strange to think of it. It had been months since he had been here, but it felt like yesterday. Everything was as he had left it. The space was quite small, but was considered roomy compared to many cargo freighter barracks. There was a comfortable bunk, raised above a decent sized desk with a good quality chair. All the walls were compartmentalized into shallow closet space, holding his few possessions. He could go inside and sit at his desk, and it would be as if nothing had happened. But of course that was not possible. He shook his head as if to physically rid himself of such wasteful thinking, and continued along the corridor.

"All good, chief?" asked Brother Anderson.

"Yeah, fine. Solid," replied Colin as if he understood the doctor to be asking about the structural integrity of his quarters. He knew full well that he had truly been referring to his own internal structural integrity - his feelings of safety and confidence. Of course he was worried. There was a very good chance they would all end up as space dust before long. All the more reason to focus on the task at hand.

Brother Anderson knew too that Colin's answer was part bluff. It was why he had worded his question just so, to give Colin that slim opportunity, that double entendre, to at once both reveal and protect his inner universe. The subtle vagaries of language could be sharp instruments of healing. They were both the scalpel and the suture, getting at the root of issues and tying up ugly wounds. This was an area where Brother Anderson excelled, and it was as much a result of his chaplaincy training as his medically based psychological studies.

Brother Anderson's original programming had been purely medical. He was a doctor first and foremost. He always would be. The medical programming was base level. It had become a lens that influenced all subsequent learning, and even re-programming. He tended to think of everything as an issue of optimal health, even now as CSO, he thought of, and acted for the sake of, the "health" of the ship. The chaplaincy programming had dovetailed well into this paradigm, as it had been focused primarily on the spiritual well-being of the crew. In fact, large portions of the programming were nearly parallel to his previously installed counselling programming, just with a lot of the language changed for some of the same concepts. He had found that in practical usage, much of the jargon was interchangeable. He was able to implement concepts from either discipline with the lingo of the other, tailoring a conversation to utilize a finely nuanced lexiconic mix of spiritual and physically based words, customized to each client depending on their background and receptivity to certain conceptual leanings. This allowed him to minimize discomfort, even when discussing difficult and painful subjects. Intentional language could at once both anesthetize and cure the wounded psyche. And all psyches had wounds. Some were fresh and on the surface. A recent traumatic experience needed to be grappled with psychologically or it could expand. Oftentimes it may tear rifts between people - families, crew. More often it could fracture a man - part of him withdrawing into a dark corner in search of shelter from further injury. Patterns of unresolved pain built up a shell around a person to keep others away - to keep out the risk.

"This is the spot, Chief." Brother Anderson stopped moving. They were half-way down corridor D-1, the central thoroughfare of sector D, a wide hallway designed to accommodate easy passage in both directions for crew and equipment. There was nothing visibly present to indicate anything particular about this spot. The wall panels were identical in appearance all the way down the corridor, and pretty much the same throughout the ship. Colin habitually glanced at his wrist. Normally, his comm band would have confirmed the correct position, but of course, he was not wearing it now. It didn't matter. He knew the doctor was right. He looked behind and ahead down the corridor, eyeballing its length. This was the spot for sure, halfway down the main corridor would coincide with halfway down the support structure, the spot of maximum concentration for the mechanical stresses they had seen on-screen.

Deftly removing a wall panel, Colin revealed a diagonal section of strutwork. He removed three more panels, opening up a large section of wall. After pulling out several layers of insul-matt, it was now clear that the struts formed a 'W' shape, with cabling snaking through several access tubes built into each strut at regular intervals. Behind them was more insul-matt and, presumably, the backside of another wall panel. If he recalled correctly, the space behind it was occupied by a few small office cubicles, for admin staff that were "annexed" after the main admin workspace was completely occupied. At the top of the wall Colin could make out the bottom flange of the corner beam. These larger beams were what they really needed to be dealing with. The forces were transferred along their length by the vibrational patterns. He removed a ceiling panel, then glanced around stupidly.

"Forgot to bring a ladder," he mumbled. "Um, I don't suppose you could boost me up, Doc?"

Brother Anderson complied wordlessly, taking a wide based kneeling stance, and held out a hand as a step. The other arm he held out and up in half of an old-fashioned "field-goal" position. Colin placed a foot on Brother Anderson's hand, gripped his other arm, and deftly hoisted himself up, his head now almost reaching the ceiling.

"OK - a little higher please." Colin's head slowly poked up into the ceiling cavity as Brother Anderson easily lifted Colin's weight in one hand. Colin's cry of "Whoa! - good there!" indicated when it was high enough. He took a lamp from his toolbelt and spent about a minute squirming around, trying to get a decent look from a few angles, then swung himself down.

"Yeah. Well, there's not much room up there."

"It doesn't appear to be very conducive to additional bracing," agreed Brother Anderson.

"Still, let's leave these panels off for now. Maybe we'll think of something."

They both doubted it.

"Well, let's take a look at B and C sectors. See where we're at with that." Colin started off slowly. He choked down a strong feeling of disappointment. This was really bad. The obvious conclusion was somehow more real to him, now that he had seen with his own eyes the impossibility of their hopeful idea.

The far bow end of sector D contained the assembly room on the starboard side, and, to port, the mess hall, whose entrance they now approached. As they neared the hatch a quiet whistling sound could be heard, which upon inspection, was caused by airflow through a small crack in the floor.

They both stared.

"Shit," said Colin.

"Both this corridor and the mess hall appear to have normal air pressures, but there is a slight gradient between the two. I believe this air is coming from the mess hall Chief. Shall we go inside?"

"Open it" responded Colin, gesturing with his head toward the hatch. It slid open normally, with no sudden bursts of air, fire, explosions, or anything. They entered the mess hall.

Sure enough, the crack in the floor continued in the mess hall for another three meters or so. Colin stared at it with a feeling that was a mix of terror and amazement. He didn't even notice the blackened epoxy carapaces. Until he did.

"What the fuck!" He jumped backward, startled, tripping over his own legs and stumbling to the cracked floor. "What the hell are those? Are those BODIES?" he stammered.

"Oh! - I'm sorry! I forgot to warn you!" Brother Anderson stammered back. Yes, it would have been a good idea to give him a heads up about this. Colin only stared, but his stare alternated every few seconds between the rows of his deceased crewmates left to rot out in the open with nothing but a clear plexi-coating, and this idiot robot standing over him, now in charge of the ruined ship.

"This is insane!" he finally sputtered, "What have you done? Why are these here?" He was more than a little perplexed as to what had prompted the decision to treat these bodies this way, but his curiosity was easily eclipsed by his anger. The dead should not be dishonored like this. In space, there's always the problem of burial, of course, but a respectful "float" was fine, as long as there was a bit of ceremony to it. A few honoring words, some sentiment, and a clean goodbye. But this? This was just - wrong. And for God's sake, the chaplain of all people should know as much.

"Colin. I understand you are upset."

Colin glared, ready to argue if necessary, but resigned to at least give the robot a chance to answer his question. He was a practical man. He figured a question deserved an answer, even if it was intended rhetorically.

"The initial casualties were given a proper Christian funeral service, then were sealed and launched as per standard protocols."

Colin nodded involuntarily, and relaxed a little.

"Your co-workers, Scranton and Tommy were very well spoken of by the rest of the engineering team. You had a fine department there. A good team, and a good chief"

Colin responded well to the compliment, calming visibly. He was the sort of man who took his work and his team personally even as a common member of ordinary rank. A compliment to one of his team-mates or their processes, equipment, or the ship herself, was considered a compliment to him as well.

"Later on, once it was determined that a large-scale infection was in play, our options become limited.

You may not know that quarantine protocols demand that bodies are to be sealed and kept on board."

Colin had not known that fact. He nodded again slowly.

"As I was focusing on medical procedures and trying to save the lives of the crew, I had volunteers assisting with some of the other protocol procedures, including cadaver processing. Soon though, they could not keep up with the demand, and also ran out of stowage space, so I instructed them to switch to these cruder methods of sealing that you see now. This was necessary to contain the foreign microbes. And it is a standard fallback protocol."

"And then your volunteers got sick too."

"Yes, but ultimately, the ship is now safe. Completely free of contamination."

"How can you be sure?"

"Well. The contagion spread very quickly. Much faster than anything I've seen, so it outpaced the atmospheric scrubbing that kicked in as part of the protocols. But later, when it had run its course and consumed the available host pool, the germination rate slowed, and eventually the scrubbers caught up and cleaned up the air. Also there's the fact that Hannah survives, as do you."

"She's in an oxygen mask, though."

"But she wasn't yesterday."

"What?"

"Well, I suppose not technically yesterday. I placed Hannah under oxygen approximately thirty-three hours ago. Until then, she had been breathing quite freely."

"What?! But how?"

"As you may have noticed, Hannah has always had a rather reclusive nature, and often sequestered herself in her studio for days at a time, working on her musical projects. This was the case during the calamities of hull breach and subsequent viral outbreak. She was completely oblivious to any of the events onboard. Once quarantine protocols began, her airlock was disabled and she was trapped in her quarters, but she still did not realize it until almost a week later, when her local food cache became depleted and she tried to go for a supply run. At that point I accompanied her here to the mess hall, where she has been residing ever since, as evidenced by her detritus." he waved toward a large scattered collection of Omega Bar wrappers.

Colin glanced around the mess hall. Sure enough, the wrappers, and a few bottles backed up the doctor's story. They were roughly piled up in one corner, in front of him to the left. There was a space of about fifteen feet between that spot and the nearest corpse. The food dispenser and the restrooms were across on the other side of the room. Between them lay a veritable minefield of corpses. She would have had to traverse this chilling scene every day. Colin found it hard to imagine the horror Hannah must have felt each day, every moment - living in this inescapable graveyard, surrounded always by death - decay always present, always visible.

Brother Anderson noticed Colin's gaze, his facial expression and the sudden tension in his body. "It's quite safe, I assure you. The epoxy is quite strong and completely impervious."

Colin turned his gaze to the robot. "That's not what I was worried about. Although, now that you bring that up, it may be safe for now, but it won't last long. Look at this." He pointed at the crack in the floor near his feet, then swept his arm in the direction of its line, continuing his sweeping gesture past its end and right toward the carapaces. They were right in line with the crack. Actually, it was worse. Even if the crack altered course and did not continue in a relatively straight line, it was almost certain to run into one of the carapaces, given the way they were spread practically all across the room.

"Come now," Brother Anderson countered the implication, "the crack is really nowhere near them. Why it would have to triple in size to become a danger!"

"Yes," agreed Colin, "and hasn't it already tripled in size? Hasn't it already *millioned* in size since it started out with length equals zero?"

"Well..."

"It could easily triple again in... when? In a day? In an hour?"

The two looked at each other, the realization sinking in. Surely the remains were still infectious. The doctor knew it for a fact, but even the engineer knew it instinctively. If the crack did reach one of the carapaces, the seal would be broken, the quarantine would be breached, the air would be contaminated, and the last two humans on board would be infected and killed.

Chapter 29

Hannah awoke feeling better than she had in a long time. Her head was clear, she was not tired or angry, but her stomach was growling fiercely. She looked around and recognized the med bay, then had a foggy recollection of how she had come to be here. "Stupid!" she accused herself.

She got up and took a quick survey of the surroundings in the hopes of finding an Omega Bar, but, finding none, she retrieved her clothing from a drawer and got dressed. That was actually fairly depressing, since her clothes were disgustingly dirty. They had a certain stiff gritty feel, which seemed to transfer to her body as she put them on, and she was overcome with a strong desire to bathe. There was a shower in med bay, but she really needed clean clothes. She had not thought earlier to pursue the idea. Depression tends to drain a person of the will to bother trying anything. Her own unwillingness to acknowledge her emotions had led her into a downward spiral, but waking up today felt like a fresh start. She needed to do this. She *needed* clean clothes. For the sake of her health. Brother Anderson would *have to* help her. But that meant she would have to *ask* him to.

"Crap!"

She hated the thought. Her mother had said that she was "unable to hold a civil conversation". She had not said it accusingly. It was a matter of fact. Hannah actually was incapable of having a civil conversation. At least, that's what the evidence of historical conversation seemed to indicate. Other than Suzzanne, and Cherise before her,

Hannah could not think of anyone who she had really ever talked to. Well, technically, that was not true. She had had many discussions with her childhood oboe instructors and her record producers, but those conversations had always been purely technical. The music needed to be a certain way, and that certain way needed to be discussed and refined, which required the exchange of details regarding those refinements. The muse was pragmatic. Hannah's own opinion did not really enter into it. Those technical details seemed to be delivered to her mind, and the minds of her instructors and producers, through some immediate divine agency. Inspiration was not a matter of taste. It was a compulsive servitude. They were simply slaves of the music that somehow existed already in some immaterial state, like the mythical statue magically controlling the will of the sculptor to free its predestined shape from the raw stone.

The "*shoosh*" sound of the med bay hatch pulled her from her thoughts as the robot doctor entered the room, accompanied by the gentle whirring of his wheels and whatever internal mechanisms fueled them. But another distinct sound unblended and came into focus two seconds later. Footsteps. Human footsteps. She whirled toward the door in time to see a male figure momentarily framed in stunning partial silhouette.

Her mind raced. A flash of hazy memory saved roughly during stoned inebriation - a figure lying in a bed. Her head whipped around; yes, that bed was empty now - empty but unmade, the blanket and sheet hanging sloppily. Someone had been there. The memory had not lied. Yet, words echoed through her head belying a contradictory assumption - a robotic voice: "the crew is dead, everyone is dead, we are alone".

"Oh, Hannah. Good, I'm glad you are awake." said that same lying robotic voice, this time not merely a memory in her mind.   Looking up, there was the robot. He claimed to be a doctor, a priest, a ship captain, a friend. He claimed many things. None of them were true. Here stood a machine, a manipulator, a liar.

And behind him, behind this robot who had told her that everyone was dead, stood a man. A man, clearly not dead. A man, clearly a crewman from engineering, by the uniform. As he moved out of silhouette her focus adjusted to his face, and recognition dawned, seeing through four months of beard growth. This was a man she knew. A man for whom she felt a hatred twice as strong as the loathing she held for the lying robot. A man named Colin. A man who had molested her friend.

"Unbelievable," Hannah muttered to herself in an ironically deadpan tone. A curious mix of anger, betrayal, frustration, dread, and helplessness resulted in a strange emotional cancellation. These emotions were inseparable in her mind though. There was no room for self-analysis, even if she had been the introspective type. Her body moved of its own accord now, stiffly but quickly circling the long way around the room, seeking a route toward the door which maximized her distance from the room's other occupants. She felt as though she watched the scene separated from her body, through red clouds of fog smudging and obscuring space, time, and personality. There were no more people; simply anonymous objects slowly floating in a graceful, silent circle. She felt no pain as a fist slammed into a medical monitoring device, sending shards of plas-screen skittering across the room. Somewhere, someone's foot lashed out in a rather clumsily performed dropkick, connecting with the stand of another rather expensive looking medical device, hurling it against the wall with an impressive flash of sparks. As she ran from the fog-shrouded room, she heard her own voice echoing in a muffled shriek; "... stuck here with a fucktard robot liar and a lying rapist!"

Chapter 30

Hannah stared at the small dark spot on the mess hall wall. She stood in the middle of the room, having entered moments ago. As she caught her breath, she barely remembered storming out of med bay or running through the corridors. She didn't notice the stack of panels leaning up beside an exposed wall section in corridor D-1. She didn't notice the crack in the floor that had appeared since she was last in this room. She didn't notice that the vibrations of the ship were getting worse. She didn't notice the streaks of blood that still oozed slowly from her knuckles and stained her fingers. She did, however, notice several empty Roth's bottles on the floor near her, and these she kicked across the room with an impressive measure of strength and a certain kind of dumb luck in terms of accuracy. The first bottle flew like an arrow, directly at another bottle, also empty, that stood proudly on the counter near the dispenser. Both bottles smashed spectacularly. The next kick sent another bottle sailing directly toward the dispenser. Halfway through its flight her subconscious took note of the trajectory and its possible negative effects. Time seemed to slow, as the bottle continued to spin carelessly along its path. The narrow end smashed squarely into and through the dispenser's display screen. The crash was accompanied by a sparking sound as the circuitry fried itself. The mess hall lights went out, draping the mess hall in utter blackness. A second later, the emergency lights kicked on, but the single dim red lamp above the hatch emitted only enough light to show the exit path, not to light the room.

"Shit!"

She started to run toward the dispenser, tripping over something in the darkness, then made her way a bit more slowly, bumping into a couple of carapaces along the way. She managed to ignore them. The dispenser was for the most part unresponsive, save for a faint, pathetically distorted beep of failure when she tried to enter any commands. A small wisp of smoke wafted out of the machine, bringing with it a horrible smell that made her feel a bit sick. At the same time though, she felt a hunger pang, as her body instinctively recognized the implication of the broken dispenser and had relayed the bad news to her stomach directly, bypassing her conscious mind.

She leaned against the dispenser. And sobbed. The dispenser had been the last thing she could trust to take care of her. Inexplicably, it suddenly seemed to act as a stand-in for her mother, now departed, and never really grieved. She had not said goodbye. She had not fully accepted the hard truth. "Everyone is dead" was somehow a much easier concept to process than "my mother is dead." The impact of this realization shook Hannah to a depth she did not recognize and would never have guessed could exist. Some deep buried cavern of emotion never explored was suddenly flooded as if by a great wave. Her body racked in great heaving wails as tears soaked her cheeks. She had never known such pain. The torment of this loss was a tangible yet shapeless thing. It surrounded her like a heavy blanket, muffling her thought, her breath, her very life.

Eventually, Hannah slept. Pain turned to numbness, and numbness to oblivion. Hours passed. Maybe days. Her subconscious mind slowly fermented fear and anger into sorrow. Her anguish became a well-worn cloak of blackness and silent sound. That impossible sound emanated from a hidden seed within Hannah's psyche. It ebbed with her choking breaths. It wove a resonance between her pulse and the white noise of her unfathomable neural rhythms. Slowly, as Hannah let the pain of loss and trauma emerge and flow uninhibited, the dark blanket transformed its mass into sharp energy.

Periodic bursts of uncontrollable sobbing gradually became interspersed with deeply exhaled sighs. These sighs gradually moved from her chest to include nose and throat, instigating first her sinus to a tingling energetic sensation, then her larynx to engage a passive voice, allowing each sigh to become a small vocalization, a humming buzz, a primordial word stripped of semantic limits and thus containing all possible meaning.

Eventually, this humming took on tone, and the tone became a wandering melody. An improvisational tune of remembrances of human connectivity. It gradually resolved into a very specific song of remembrance, of mothers singing sweet little homemade lullabies to their young daughters.

"Little babe, blessed babe, there's nothing to fear, so sleep my dear."

Chapter 31

Colin looked at Brother Anderson, then the hatch through which Hannah had stormed out, then the wrecked medical equipment and their splintered pieces. He had no idea what they were for, but he knew they looked expensive. He looked back at Brother Anderson.

"Shouldn't we go after her?"

"Definitely not."

"That looks like blood there, doesn't it? - She's hurt." He nodded at the splinters. Indeed, there were several drops of blood among them.

"Yes, it is. But… It is most likely superficial lacerations. Still..." he hesitated. "I'm continuing to monitor her vital signs as usual. If there is substantial blood loss, I will know."

It seemed a bit strange. Why such hesitation? It almost seemed as though the doctor was afraid of this girl. Not without good reason. Colin certainly recognized her fury, and he felt no small trepidation himself, but for a robot to feel it; wasn't that impossible?

"Umm, well. I'm gonna head down to engineering for a bit."

"Very good, chief. Call me if you need anything."

"Will do. Oh, are comms actually working? They came up yellow on my scan."

"Partially, yes. The link in engineering appears to be active. Call me when you get there just to be sure."

"10-4," Colin joked.

Leaving medbay he hesitated, then turned left - the opposite direction from engineering. Walking a few meters down the corridor, he visually scanned the floor for drops of blood. There was one. A few more meters. Nothing. The doctor was right; the bleeding wasn't serious. Still, he felt he should go after Hannah. It didn't seem right to just leave her alone. Perhaps he could help her somehow. But how? Perhaps Brother Anderson was right about that too. She hated him. How would she like it if he were to follow her? That would just upset her even more. Resignedly, he turned toward engineering deck.

Chapter 32

Brother Anderson stood outside the mess hall. He could not bring himself to open the hatch. "She's fine," he told himself for the hundredth time. "Her pulse is normal, her breathing sounds clear and relaxed. Her temperature just slightly cooler than average." These were really the only vital signs he could track indirectly. He could do so from anywhere on the ship. Yet here he was standing by the mess hall hatch. Despite the available evidence, he was concerned for her. As his patient, he truly did have her health in mind. She had been asleep a long time. Way too long. It felt weird.

He triggered the hatch and it slid open with a faint scratching sound, as opposed to its usual smooth whoosh. He looked at the crack in the floor. Yes, it had grown. The room was moving slightly out of alignment, causing the hatch to scratch against its sill. The sound, however small, was not inaudible to a perceptive ear. Hannah heard it subconsciously. Her breathing halted for a second, and she turned over in her sleep. In the poorly lit room, Brother Anderson relied on his infrared vision, which allowed him to note the sudden rush of warmth to the left side of her forehead, which until moments ago had been pressed against the hard floor. In normal lighting, this spot would now have been clearly visible as a red splotch on her face, a crescent lock of dark hair draped clumsily across it.

She could really use a pillow. Yes. Brother Anderson decided to get her one. Had she really lived all this time in the mess hall without one? He was a fool for not thinking of this before. He turned, and allowed the door to shut behind him, moving back along the corridor, back toward med bay to retrieve a pillow and a blanket. Along the way he derided himself. Hannah had claimed that he did not care about her. He now saw that the evidence had proved her to be right. He had left her alone in a cold room without a pillow for months. No pillow, no blanket. Just hard picnic tables and a basic washroom. A bare floor and all the food she could ever want was about all the luxury he had afforded her. But it wasn't even a bare floor really. Not bare at all. It was littered with the corpses of her fellow man.

Brother Anderson was in fact a terrible person. Had he possessed tear ducts, he may have wept at the realization.

Chapter 33

Colin tinkered with the comms systems. Several of the circuits were dead; most likely due to blown amplifiers, but since most of the ship was now unoccupied, he saw no reason not to steal a few components from the unneeded sections to repair the sections that mattered. One such component made a small spark as he unplugged it, and he hoped it wasn't damaged. He routed it through to the med bay circuit and gave Brother Anderson a call to test it.

"Hello Colin."

"OK good - just testing something."

"Alright, is there anything else I can do?"

"Hmm no, not right... Oh! Well actually, yes. I'm looking at the comms subsystems maps here. Have you used the long range comms lately by any chance?"

"No. We are still in the comms shadow."

"Yeah that's what I figured. Well, maybe I'll give it a couple fresh parts just in case. Can't afford any trouble with that one."

"Very good, Chief."

"Oh, and how long you figure until we come out of the shadow?"

"At our current velocity, it should be about another five or six days."

That was good news. Colin knew very well that the vast majority of the flight of the Ventas-341 was made in the radio shadow. She travelled deep within asteroid belts, behind billions of tons of rock. It was safe enough. They stuck to well defined linear channels, naturally clear of debris due to their particular orbital distance. Colin had been along this particular route enough times to know that it was a roughly six month journey from the load-up back to the civilized world of comms. Back to data streaming, and links to home; back to decent entertainment. By his math, calculating the time he'd been asleep, and the time before the crash, and now adding about a week according to Brother Anderson's estimates, that would mean they were more or less still on course. The ship drifted along in a regular orbit just like everything else not acted upon by other outside forces. She used no thrust, once up to cruising speed. But he had been worried about the collisions. Hull breaches could generate thrust as pressurized atmosphere escaped. To say nothing of explosive fires and the like. He had only a basic intuition of these facts though. He could not begin to speculate on the magnitude of such forces. Would they have been enough to throw the Ventas off course? Surely not, he reasoned with himself. A fully loaded freighter had so much inertia going for her it would take a huge effort to bump her off course even slightly. Still, he had worried. Just another thing floating around in the back of his mind. But he felt better now, knowing. They were still on course - and they were nearing civilized radio-space.

Back to the task at hand; Colin finished the planning for his next stage of troubleshooting, flagged a select few of the more important circuits with a Jiffy Marker, then began working his way through the repetitive steps of actually replacing and unit testing various components. It was not rocket science, and he soon found his mind drifting.

He imagined himself, floating in a spacesuit, driving a thruster-tug, surrounded by tiny virus-piloted fluorine-lattice matrix-ships. His giant hand closing in around one of them, grasping it between finger and thumb like some kind of enormous demigod, and examining it with all-knowing vision.

"How does one capture a speck of pure volatility?" the demigod mused.

The virus-pilot removed its helmet and, shaking her head, loosed waves of shoulder-length black hair. She gazed upon the demigod, and in a panicked instant, briefly clawed at the matrix-ship's emergency jettison lever, before transforming into a calm, rational lattice of steel reinforced hexagonal panels that suddenly grew to a size which dwarfed even the demigod himself. Its giant silver virus head perched atop a pair of kneeling humanoid legs with wheels embedded in the joints. Laser eyes drilled into his own.

"The ions repel each other," said the virus. "So a lattice of halogens is impossible!"

"Unless there were some even stronger force!" Colin's own voice boomed through his daydream and into the metallic surroundings of the engineering bay.

"Shit! The doc was right. Maybe I do need some rest." Colin set down his tools on the workbench, and began walking slowly toward… where was he going? Med bay? His own quarters? He wasn't sure. He just let his body walk. His mind was already half asleep. Yet it mused:

If only she weren't so deadly, so angry.

Chapter 34

Brother Anderson felt an odd sense of excitement. He did not recall experiencing this feeling before. Perhaps he had not. He would have to check his extended memory records. And soon he could. This was in fact the source of his excitement. Soon the ship would be back in comms range. Soon he would regain his tanglebase connection.

"The tanglebase" was the colloquial term for the galactic data cloud. It was the multiply redundant, distributed, and parallel web of corporate, personal, and governmental data. It was the sum total of all human data. Not knowledge, mind you. The tanglebase was all about the raw data. As humanity's reach expanded, her data resources had multiplied exponentially. Ironically, within the vast expanse of space, connectivity had taken a giant step backwards, and local asynchronous computation was required now more than ever. But even so, all the worlds' data resource providers had merged long ago, and in so doing, had enabled a single de-duplicated polydimensional compression and encryption scheme that allowed ultra-fine grain access control to every living human. Not that it really made much difference. It's not like the world was really a better place because of it. Everyone knew everything, but people continued to act as ignorant as ever. And the free access didn't last long. It was only after a couple of decades that corporate deregulation and greed led back to a monopolizing trend, through incremental price hikes, until most of humanity was again excluded from access. Now their data was the domain of the rich - or the highly technical. There were always workarounds for the highly technical; one just had to keep up with the ever-evolving APIs. Brother Anderson could hardly wait to reconnect and get back up to speed on those advancements. He also had a huge backlog of personal data he wanted to revalidate. The current feeling of anticipation was only one such example. His on-ship storage was finite. Much of his prior mind had been left tangle-side only upon entering the shadow just over a year ago. And with his augmented mind now occupying the ship's full availability, he had so much to explore, to springboard off from. He was root bound and the feeling of a tensioned spring was beginning to grate on his nerves. He needed to break these bounds.

Chapter 35

Colin had a fitful sleep. He tossed and turned, tormented by subconscious half-dreams. The virus-pilot was back, this time looking sexier than before, but armed with an assault rifle. She rolled down the side window of her lattice car, leaned out and turned the gun on him. As she pulled the trigger, words came out of the rifle, "*the ions repel each other.*" it said.

He twitched violently awake, banging his head against the wall of his bunk. He was drenched with sweat. He still had his coveralls and boots on. A blanket was tangled around his leg. It tripped him up as he attempted to wrest himself from the clutches of his bed.

There was a knock on his hatch. Brother Anderson's voice followed.

"Colin, are you awake? May I come in?"

"Yeah sure."

The hatch opened. Brother Anderson stepped in and handed Colin an Omega Bar.

"How are you feeling, Colin?"

"Umm, fine I guess. I just had a super-weird dream."

"Really?"

"Yeah, but it's nothing." Colin hesitated.

"Alright. I would be interested to hear it anyway," the robot offered.

"Well, OK. You know that virus-lattice thing? I was wondering, what if you tried to somehow capture one?"

"That would be very difficult to do, I'm afraid."

"Yeah, I know. You would need some kind of containment field or something, to prevent it from reacting with whatever you touch it with, right?"

"Correct."

"Plus if we wanted to do that we would have to turn the ship around and travel for four months to get back to that spot where the stuff was."

"Roughly, yes."

"And we obviously can't do that."

"Obviously."

"Did you even think about trying to grab a sample, while we were still close to it, or grab some of the stuff that came through the hull?"

"Well… I didn't really consider it much. After all, we don't have any containment field generators on board do we?"

"Well, no. Not in so many words."

"What do you mean?"

"I dunno. It's stupid. Just makes me wonder is all. It's like nothing you've ever seen you said, right? The stuff must be worth a fortune. It's just kindof a shame that's all." Colin gazed off at nothing in particular. The idea of missing such a valuable opportunity bothered him. But there was really nothing to be done about it. They were going to have enough trouble staying on course and limping the ship home without adding any further complications and wasting a lot of time doing it. The reality of the situation was actually quite dire. Once they came past the asteroid belt, they would need to perform a navigational maneuver. The standard shipping lane zone branched off and their route required a thirty degree course correction; it would be a hard acceleration, and with fifty million tons of cargo, required some serious thrust to pull off. The forces involved could easily tear the weakened and already unstable ship in half. 'Could,' he thought to himself. That's an understatement alright. I wonder what the probabilities are. '50/50' he joked to himself, and chuckled a little out loud. Brother Anderson looked at him but said nothing. Colin decided the joke was good enough to share, even if he would have to explain the punchline.

"Back in engineering school, I had to take probability and statistics - never did get the hang of it - I don't know how I even passed the exam. They must have been grading on the curve."

Brother Anderson nodded.

"Anyway, I was just thinking - what are the chances the ship rips in half during the course correction maneuvers? Gotta be 50/50 right? It either does or it doesn't!" He laughed at himself, fully aware of his faulty logic.

Brother Anderson wished he could laugh. Not because he found it funny, but because he understood that laughter was an excellent form of relational cement, and that in such a situation it would help to ease Colin's anxiety. Instead, he chose the closest option.

"Ah yes, that's clever!" he lied.

Colin looked down at his hands, subconsciously trying to distract himself from this line of reasoning. It was no use.

"We aren't going to make it, are we?"

"We can't know that for certain."

"Not for certain, no. But look - this turn is typically what? - a 3G burn?" He stood now, rising from the bunk and turning with his finger in the air, tracing a curve in his mind to simulate the ship's trajectory.

"With those kind of forces, in her condition, she'll never hold together.

Brother Anderson remained silent, though he knew Colin's words to be true. Even as he listened to Colin speak, he was running and re-running simulations and scenarios, crunching numbers, calculating probabilities.

"Look," Colin continued, "I know we can't ditch the cargo, even if it would save the ship. I know we can't just give up. Even if we are the only crew left, we still have a job to do, and ultimately that job is to deliver our cargo. I know we've got to try it." He sighed. "We just better come up with a pretty damn good backup plan for when it all goes south."

"Agreed."

"So we're gonna need to ready up a nice comfy escape pod, and check the local maps - Where's a good place to crash around here?" He chuckled.

"Shall we go to med bay? I can pull up some nav charts on the big screen."

"Yeah, I guess. It's just..." Colin hesitated.

Brother Anderson waited a moment. "What is it, Colin? I know you are feeling anxious. I want you to know you can talk to me about anything."

"Yeah, I know... I mean, after all you're my chaplain, right? It's just... It's Hannah. I mean, I feel like she should have a say in some of these plans."

"Ideally, yes. But she refuses to cooperate, Colin."

"Look - she's just been through a lot and she doesn't know what to do."

"I know that Colin. I'm her chaplain too. And her doctor."

"Well, yeah, exactly! Can't you see she's totally freaking out?"

"Of course I can see that."

"Well?!"

"I'm not sure what else to say, Colin. I have done whatever I could. She really doesn't want anything to do with me. I believe she has something against robots in general."

"I guess she has something against a lot of things in general. But we can't just leave it at that. It's not right. We have to try to help her. I just wish I could go talk to her."

"Maybe you can."

"Not a good idea."

"She hates you. Why?"

"Ugh, well… There was this stupid thing that happened, but it doesn't really make sense. I didn't do anything really."

"Colin. What happened?"

"Ah crap. OK. So it's about Hannah's friend Suzzanne."

"I know her."

"Yeah and there may have been a fair bit of alcohol involved."

"I'm not here to judge you, Colin. Perhaps if I know the whole story, we can work together to figure out a way to work through the issues."

"Yeah. So the thing is, I literally didn't do anything. I was standing there talking to my buddies. It was Friday night and they had the mess hall converted into a dance club like they do. Lots of people were dancing and it was really noisy ad whatever but I was just trying to have a couple beers with my friends. We were just joking around and whatever. Tommy - you know Tommy right? - well, he is a little crazy even sober, but he had a few drinks in him and he starts horsing around like he does and shoves me into these girls who are dancing beside where we're standing. I dropped my beer and it splashed everywhere - I guess it got on those girls. It was Hannah's friend Suzzanne and Stef from navs. They started screaming and Suzzanne fell on the floor. I tried to help her up but Stef and some other girl were pushing me away, plus Tommy was grabbing at me and hooting like an idiot. Anyway, when he pushed me into them and I dropped my beer, I instinctively raised my arms in front of me to catch myself, right? And I guess when I smashed into them, my elbow might have hit Stef in the face. Well, I know it did, because I definitely felt it connect, and I heard that click of her jaw snapping shut. It gave me a sick feeling to think I had just hit a woman. And also I apparently touched Suzzanne's chest with my other arm I guess. But like, obviously it was an accident. And I felt terrible about it and I was trying to apologize and to help them but they were just pushing me away and yelling. But then then next day Scranton asked me about it cuz Tynor told him that he heard that I tried to grab Suzzanne's breast. So I guess according to Suzzanne, I like purposefully tried to feel her up, which is ridiculous, but of course Hannah is going to believe whatever Suzzanne tells her. It's not like she was there to see it. And as far as I can figure, that's why Hannah has a grudge against me."

"I see." replied Brother Anderson. After a few seconds, he continued, "I supposed it would be best for me to talk to her about this and see if I can clear up any misconceptions she may have - explain that it was all an accident."

"Yes! Could you?"

"Unfortunately, no."

“What do you mean? No?! It was your idea!”

“I mean, I should, but I can’t.”

“Why not?”

“Well, to be honest, she doesn’t trust me any more than she does you. She would not be open to having a conversation with me. The sad truth is that I have not done a particularly good job as a chaplain toward her, and my actions or lack thereof have contributed to her having a rather poor opinion of me. I was just pondering this before I came to see you this morning, in fact, and I have come to the conclusion that it is imperative to my duty as both her chaplain and her doctor to try to somehow rebuild and regain Hannah’s trust.”

“How will you do that?”

“That is what I need to figure out.”

Chapter 36

Hannah felt like shit. It was not the sort of shitty feeling that comes from a hangover. It was partly the sort of shitty feeling that you get when you are surrounded by assholes and everyone who ever meant anything to you is dead, and it was partly the sort of shitty feeling you get when you realize that you yourself are also an asshole and you recognize that part of you is also dead and maybe the rest should be as well.

She sat there for a long time, just feeling it. Then, suddenly, she bored of it and decided to do something different. She picked herself up off the ground and gave the dispenser an awkward sort of hug.

"This is for you, mom," she whispered to the dispenser. Then slowly and carefully in the half dark, using her foot as a makeshift broom, she swept up the broken shards of bottle and dispenser into a neat pile, and pushed it up against the wall, out of the way. She then began to collect up the dozens of Omega Bar wrappers that littered the room.

As she worked, she hummed quietly, matching tones with the creaking and roaring sounds emanating from the ship. It was a game she had enjoyed as a child, finding the exact frequency, and then altering her own tone ever so slightly higher or lower so that her voice formed a throbbing beat frequency with the original signal, the interference patterns creating a slow rhythm whose frequency was the difference between the two primary sources. The sounds of the ship were a constantly changing subtlety. Groans, underlay shimmies atop the always present rumbles. These were the classic spaceship sounds. Now though there were other sounds. A deep rhythmic thudding that she tried to ignore as it did not play well into her game, and a series of relatively high pitched squeals. The squeals were in the right range for the game, and were an excellent challenge, as their tone rose and fell a bit too fast to allow time for an easy pitch match. She had to constantly adjust in order to maintain the interference. The game now required more of her attention, so she stopped picking up trash for the moment. For a few minutes, the squeals continued to rise, both in pitch and volume. Then, suddenly, with a tumultuous screech added in, they reached a fever pitch like an orchestral climax - and the emergency lighting failed, plunging her into total darkness.

The shriek ended in a nerve-grating metallic tearing sound, after which many of the higher pitched whines died out, leaving only a multilayered tapestry of low rumbles and an odd whistling wind. Far away, an alarm klaxon rang out at even intervals. A few bangs and pings reverberated through the walls and floor like a struck bell.

In the darkness she noticed the rhythm of her own pulse, though her perception of it was more a feeling than a hearing, it seemed to course past her eardrums, her eyelids, her armpits. She shut her eyes tightly, and opened them again. She waved her hand in front of her face. Not even a flicker was visible.

"Shit," she declared. "Shit, Shit, Shit."

"HELLO!"

The robot always monitored her. She had figured that out long ago. He creepily watched her every move.

"HELLOOO! It's pitch dark in here! The emergency lights went out! I can't see a fucking thing! It's NOT COOL!"

Nothing happened.

"Come on! Are you shitting me." This was said more to herself, in a low voice, almost under her breath.

"Dammit. Is he doing this on purpose?"

"FUCK YOU ROBOT!"

"WHY WON'T YOU ANSWER?"

"Oh OK sure - I get it. It's the rapist's idea."

"FUCK YOU TOO YOU FUCKIN ASSHOLE - FUCK YOU BOTH!"

A few minutes passed as she tried to think logically about the situation. This SUCKS. That robot is an asshole. But still… would he actually do this on purpose? Would he just let this happen? Could he just let this happen? He's a doctor. He's a brainless doctor. He was programmed, albeit very shittily, to protect her. He couldn't actually think. He couldn't do this even if he wanted to.

"Shit."

In a way that made it worse. That meant something was very broken. Was the robot even still alive - I mean not alive, but well, whatever - working? Maybe he was destroyed in whatever that horrible sound was. Maybe the other guy was too. It would serve him right. That fuckin' creep. Maybe they were both destroyed and she would never have to see either of those assholes ever again.

"Oh God."

Chapter 37

Colin and Brother Anderson raced down corridor E-1 amidst the strobing yellow and red emergency lighting and the blaring din of the klaxon.

They had been alerted immediately. Not like they could miss it. The sound of the ship tearing itself apart was hideous enough to wake any engineer from a dead sleep. Brother Anderson had yelled "Life Support failure on sectors C and D!" Colin had never heard a robot yell. It was a strange thing - more or less still a talking voice, but slightly sped up, and surprisingly loud, with a little bit of clipping distortion.

Up ahead, through the intersection hex, corridor D-1 loomed dark like a gaping cavern. By the looks of it, even emergency power had failed in sector D. Barely slowing his pace, Colin fumbled deftly in his tool belt for his flashlight, then clipped it on his shoulder, just as he reached the dark corridor. Colin's light bounced wildly as he ran, creating crowds of shadows that seemed to pounce from every jutting wall contour. He drove forward, chasing the beastly images as if they were his prey. He could have run no faster had these same beasts hunted him - his own life depending upon it. Just behind him, Brother Anderson wheeled on, oblivious to these imaginings, his infrared vision functioning normally. In a way though he too was running blindly. The loss of sector power disabled his regular biodata scan. Hannah had become invisible to him. One thing that was blatantly obvious was that the sector's life support was offline. It could not function without sector main power. The oxygen level would last quite a while normally, but a telltale hissing sound indicated a possible pressure leak. There was no way to guess with any accuracy how quickly air pressure would fall to dangerous levels, but they had to act fast.

"Colin, I cannot tell for certain, but the mess hall may be depressurizing. We may only have a few minutes to get Hannah out of there."

Colin managed only a grunt in reply, all his breathe spent on running, but even so, he managed to add an extra burst of speed. Within a few more seconds, he was hammering on the door sensor. Of course, the door would not open without power.

"Can you bypass this with your battery power?"

"I think so. Please remove that panel cover."

Colin smashed at it with the blunt end of a wrench, then pried it open with a flat screwdriver. Brother Anderson reached in with a pair of powered clips. A small spark was followed by the gentle whirring of an electric attenuator, then a grinding sound as the gears failed to move the door.

"It's stuck."

"SHIT!"

Hannah's face appeared at the plasglass viewpane. She appeared only slightly panicked. It was not the severe panic one would expect to see on the face of someone who was asphyxiating. She still had air at least for now, but who knows how long it would last.

"Can you hear me?!" Colin yelled through the door.

Hannah nodded.

"Take cover in the corner" he pointed to his left, "and stay low. I'm gonna blow a hole in the wall!"

He ran off toward his quarters. He remembered seeing a torch there that he technically should have returned to engineering deck long ago, and he was pretty sure he must have some kind of canned chemicals or lubricants that would be flammable or better yet, highly explosive. That kind of thing tended to wind up forgotten in his thigh pocket until he got undressed at night. Sure enough. There they were, on the floor beside his dresser. A can of 'WD-40' and one of grey spray-paint. Unsure of the exact comparative flammability properties of the two, he grabbed both. Then rummaging through a pile of junk on top of his dresser, he found the torch. It was self-sparking acetylene; perfect! Just one critical component remained - duct tape! Yes, there it was, conveniently located right beside the torch. To be fair, there had to be at least five more rolls squirrelled away at various spots in the room, but this was the only one immediately visible.

He arrived back on the scene in under two minutes.

"Still good?"

Brother Anderson nodded but then pointed the crack in the floor near the hatchway. It was quite a bit larger than the last time they had inspected it.

"It turns out, we are losing pressure on this side of the wall as well. We are down to eighty-seven percent at this location." He held two oxygen masks he had taken from a wall recess. Every primary and secondary corridor section had them. The recess hatch remained open, revealing a fire extinguisher at the ready. "I'm closing all containment hatches now."

"Good thinking. Just don't turn that oxygen on until I'm done playing with fire" he grinned. "Alright, let's get this party started!" Colin took a can in each hand and sprayed two parallel lines of paint and penetrating oil down the corridor hallway away from the door and right up to the wall near the what he guessed should correspond to the far corner of the mess hall, near the counter across from the dispenser. Colin hoped he had judged the distance correctly, but asked for a second opinion.

"This look like about the right spot, Doc?"

"Yes, that should work."

Colin used a generous amount of duct tape to hold the cans in position against the wall, in the middle of a pool of oil and paint. He peered through the viewpane pointlessly - of course, it was still pitch black - then yelled, "FIRE IN THE HOLE!"

Brother Anderson backed down the corridor quickly as Colin sparked the torch. He poised to run, then held the torch down to the oil track. It lit up beautifully, and the fire spread quickly like a wick, exactly as he had hoped. He took off down the corridor, throwing the still lit torch over his shoulder in the rough direction of the cans.

- BOOOM! -

The explosion rang through the corridor like an earthquake, knocking Colin to the floor. A pressure wave of heat rolled over him.

"Whooooaaah!" he exclaimed, then laughed uproariously even as he struggled to scramble to his feet. His ears rang with a high-pitched reverberation that drowned out his own voice; the aural equivalent to staring at the sun.

Brother Anderson was already halfway to the newly formed flaming hole in the wall, but Colin leapt passed him, boosting himself around using the robot's arm and shoulder for leverage, grabbing one of the oxygen masks from the robot's hand on his way by. Flames licked the edges of the hole, burning plastics dripping. Not bothering to try to time his move in between drips of molten wall, Colin dove into the breach, landing prone and sliding into an awkward barrel roll.

"Come on. We're running out of air!" he coaxed Hannah excitedly. She was already stepping toward him, although somewhat tenuously. He took her hand gently but firmly and led her toward the opening. Smoke was now billowing from its edges as foam dripped down the wall, the result of Brother Anderson's quick handiwork with the fire extinguisher.

"Careful," said Colin, gently applying an oxygen mask to Hannah's face, "don't breathe that smoke. It's very toxic." Hannah appreciatively put her own hand to the mask, overtop of Colin's.

For a split second, their eyes met, kindling a small spark of trust. A quiet and all-too-unfamiliar voice somewhere deep within Hannah told her "it's going to be OK."

Chapter 38

Hannah reclined on a bed in med bay, at Brother Anderson's insistence. For once she had not argued with her doctor, but allowed him to run his diagnostics. She leaned on one elbow, as the robot moved to the other bed where Colin was seated, wincing slightly as the doctor dabbed ointment onto his burns. They were small, and there were only a few. He would rather have simply ignored them, but Brother Anderson insisted on applying a disinfectant cream.

"...well, you will just have to wait a minute," the robot was telling the man. "It's too late to go in without a pressure suit now anyway, so it makes no difference."

Colin started to protest, but the robot cut him off.

"Besides, this way we can all work together to come up with a plan, instead of just running off half-cocked."

'Work together' - Colin noted the reference to their previous conversation. The robot was using his own argument against him. The realization gave him pause. He decided to shut up and go along with it. Maybe this would be a good opportunity to include Hannah in a planning discussion.

Brother Anderson continued, "Decks A through D are now inoperable and beyond repair. They must now be considered inhospitable even for simple traversing. We should be safe here in deck E, but we are going to need to gather supplies from the other decks"

"What kind of stuff do we need?" Colin asked, hoping to give Hannah a chance to jump in with ideas.

Brother Anderson was quite aware of Colin's ploy, of course, so he avoided any obvious answers, instead mentioning a true but somewhat impertinent fact; "There are some medical supplies on deck B, I think."

"What about food?" Hannah offered.

"Yeah, definitely!" encouraged Colin. "The only thing down here is a handful of protein bars, and we're almost out!" He continued, "Hannah, how much food do you think is left in the mess hall?

"Oh, tons! - I barely made a dent in the supplies."

"Oh that's excellent!" Colin answered her. It was excellent. It was excellent that there was lots of food left, although that was no surprise since half the crew had died halfway through the trip. But it was excellent also for the fact that Hannah was engaging in their conversation, and that they were taking the food supply as a shared problem for which they had a quick resolution - an easy win. This was great progress. Colin didn't bother to hide his pleasure as he gave a generous smile to both Hannah and the doctor.

"Perhaps the two of you could use the pressure suits, and make a supply run?" Brother Anderson suggested. It was too much too soon though, and Hannah became noticeably uncomfortable at the idea of being alone with Colin. "Or, we could all go." the doctor corrected himself.

Now it was Hannah's turn to shoot the doctor a knowing look. She did it subconsciously, not noticing the implications of using such human subtlety toward a robot. "I think I need to rest for a while, actually."

"Yes, of course. Actually you both should rest a while"

"It's OK," Colin argued, "I'll go." He donned the pressure suit while awkwardly avoiding looking Hannah's direction. Then, grabbing a small cart from the corner of med bay, headed for the hatch, throwing a sideways glance toward the doctor on his way past. That could have gone better, but it was a small step in the right direction. He tried not to feel disappointed. On his way through the hatch, he had a thought, and turned back.

"You like peanut butter?" he asked Hannah. It was a calculated risk.

"Um, yeah. You got some?"

"I'll see what I can do." He knew for a fact that there had to be some on board somewhere. Tommy never stopped snacking on the stuff. He headed off to find the promised confection.

"He's not such a bad guy." Brother Anderson remarked.

"God! Don't be so obvious!" Hannah retorted. Ordinarily, such a comment would have supremely pissed her off, but she was in an exceptionally fair mood, what with just having been 'rescued' and all. It was a brave thing Colin had done, blowing up a wall and leaping through fire for her. It didn't go unnoticed.

"Look, Hannah, there's something I've been meaning to say."

Hannah looked Brother Anderson square in the eyes. "Go on."

"Well, I need to apologize - that is, I want to ask you, well, It has come to my attention that I have not acted toward you in an entirely professional or even reasonable manner, and I have failed in my duties, and have lied to you."

She held her gaze.

"Can you please forgive me?" It sounded all the more strange coming from a robot.

"I'll think about it." This was not something she could process immediately. Could it even be real? Can a robot have this type of realization? She would offer a small reciprocation though, she decided. "I guess I haven't always been the nicest person to be around either."

"Well, I forgive you," said the doctor.

"OK."

Brother Anderson nodded, then turned back to his work, examining some data on a color coded console. Hannah watched for about two seconds before becoming bored. She picked up a small handheld console from the bedside table. She wasn't one to spend a lot of time logged in. She didn't enjoy games, and did not care for so called 'news', but when she was bored she would occasionally think of something. Usually a really random question. Rarely, if she was still bored and happened to be near a terminal, and not too lazy to actually bother to do it, she would actually look up that question. It just so happened that waiting in a med bay for a robot to finish scanning whatever stupid tests he was performing on you, met all three of those criteria.

Her fingerprint gained her access and opened her recent search results. Yes, they were very random indeed. A couple of definitions of words she had heard used around the ship. A couple of cocktail recipes. Some entries about various musicians; their histories, lists of recordings. She clicked on a link that caught her eye, momentarily forgetting why she was here. It failed to load. 'Right - we're in the shadow'. She then corrected herself by opening a new local network query - '*Ventas-341 crew*', which brought up a report entitled '*Current Personnel Listing.*' Not so current anymore though is it?

She scrolled through the list of names, recognizing a few. It was weird that they were all gone. The ship was full of ghosts, and those ghosts lived on in the ship's records. Or did they? She saw the record she was looking for, and clicked through. It failed to load. She tried another. Another fail.

"Say… Brother. Can I call you Brother?"

"Of course."

"Well, Brother," she giggled to herself slightly. It was a funny name for a robot. "Can I ask you a question?"

"Of course."

"I was just trying to access the ship's crew list. It's not working."

Brother Anderson smiled to himself. It wasn't a question. He wished he could say so; it was rare that he saw an opportunity to crack a joke. He couldn't risk it with Hannah though. Not yet.

"Personnel records are part of the administrative systems suite which are no longer functioning."

"Oh."

"Was there something I can help you with?"

"No, not really. I was just… curious I guess."

"About Colin?"

"What? Why would you think that?" she said, sarcastically feigning denial.

Brother Anderson just stared at her.

"Well, so… Who is this Colin, in your professional opinion? What's he like?"

"In my professional opinion? As his doctor? I can't disclose personal information."

"Oh yeah, no! Of course! I didn't mean… that. But like. I don't know. What can you tell me?"

"It is a matter of public record that Colin has worked in our engineering department for three years. After waking from a coma recently, Colin was automatically promoted to the rank of Chief Engineer."

"Chief? Ooh, la dee da!" she joked.

"It is a formality. The engineering department was left without a representative head, and he was available."

"Well that's one way of putting it I suppose."

Again the robot stared at her.

"So if he's the head of the engineering department now, who's the head of all the other departments?"

Brother Anderson became somewhat uncomfortable, but his expressionless face did not betray it. He wasn't sure he liked where the conversation was heading, and regretted mentioning Colin's promotion.

"Who is the captain? Why isn't Colin the captain?" Hannah didn't know anything about chain of command, but it seemed to her like a ship needed a captain, and if there was only one crewmember left, the honour should fall to him.

She was interrupted by a beeping from the medical console Brother Anderson had been working at.

"Ah! Your test results are ready." the doctor announced. He quickly began spouting off a series of results laced with medical jargon. Hannah began tuning him out. She already knew she was fine. Finally, the doctor concurred with her own assessment, then made to leave.

"You are fine, and free to go."

It seemed as though he wanted to get rid of her. Whatever. Hannah didn't really care. Except that there was still another matter on her mind.

"Um... One other thing, *Brother*." this time the word was laced with some sarcasm. He was acting weird.

The word 'brother' took on a twist of duality. It seemed to indicate both friend and foe, suggesting both trust and wariness.

Do you think… um, maybe when Colin gets back, you could ask him to try to find some clean clothes for me?" She hated the thought of asking for help. She hated having to rely on Colin even more. But maybe it was the only option. She really didn't know her way around the ship very well and in the state that it was in now it would be super freaky wandering around by herself. She supposed it wouldn't hurt to trust Colin for a mundane task such as this.

Chapter 39

Colin pushed the cart slowly, navigating across the mess hall between the bulbous epoxy shells. The pressure suit made his actions clumsy, and he had twice already rammed into a carapace. They were tough, and not likely to puncture by such an impact, but he took no chances. If one were to rupture… He shuddered to think of it.

His helmet light glinted off something blue and shiny, He recognized it instinctively as a large pile of foil wrappers emblazoned with a familiar logo - Omega Bars. Apparently Hannah shared his appreciation for this quick and ready nutrition source. That was great news in several ways: not only were they truly a very convenient food source which he could readily transport back to med bay, but it also gave him and Hannah something in common, which could be another small step in gaining her trust.

He finally reached the mess hall store-room. It contained a wide variety of foodstuffs, but a lot of it was suitable only for large scale food preparation. Institutional sized packages of frozen meat and vegetables, sacks of flour, sugar, rice, and other staples, five liter canisters of various sauces. One section held cases of dispenser goods - candy bars, drinks, and - yes, here we go! - Omega Bars. He loaded several cases onto the cart. It took a few more minutes of searching to track down the peanut butter, and some biscuits suitable for spreading it onto. The cart was too small to hold much else. He might have to come back for more supplies later, but there swas room for one more box. Scanning the shelves for what to choose, he had a random thought. He emptied a large box of canned goods, placing the cans directly back on the rack, then, placed the empty box onto his cart and headed back out of the mess hall, being even more careful guiding the now full cart.

Getting the loaded cart through the hole in the wall proved impossible. It had been difficult enough to get it through even unloaded. The blast hole in the wall extended nearly to the floor, but was jagged and rough, so he had been forced to unload it, drag it through, then load it back up again. Now he made his way down corridor E-1, opening up cabin hatches as he proceeded, and peering into each berth. He couldn't remember exactly which cabin had belonged to which crew member, but a quick glance jogged his memory or at least provided enough visual clues for a precursory decision. The first three he did not bother entering. The fourth bore further investigation. The room was tidy, by any standard; some may have called it immaculate. The bunk was made tightly and beside the regulation issue pillow, was a second pillow with a floral pillowcase, and a small brown teddy bear. Atop the dresser were several books and a picture of a young woman standing between an older couple. He did not recognize her, though she did look vaguely familiar. Opening the dresser drawer, he found panties and sock in the top, then t-shirts, and sweatpants in the next, and finally, two pairs of regulation coveralls in the bottom drawer. He held up a pair of coveralls, shaking out the wrinkles and letting them hang full-length. He then walked back out of the room, coveralls in hand, and checked the number of the hatch. Using the *'Jiffy Marker'* from his tool belt, he wrote that number on the tag of the coveralls, then placed them in the empty box. He repeated roughly the same process on four other berths, before proceeding down the corridor, back toward med bay.

Chapter 40

Colin returned to med bay with his cart loaded with boxes. "Omega Bars for everyone!" he exclaimed, and began piling the cases of protein bars in a corner, then added triumphantly, "aaand Peanut Butter!" He held up his arms high in the air, a jar of peanut butter in one hand and a box of biscuits in the other. These he handed to Hannah, who accepted them with a grin. He then turned back to the cart, shifting the final box to the center of the now nearly empty cart. He twisted it a few times, unthinkingly squaring the sides into alignment with the cart edges.

"There's something else," he hesitated, "for you Hannah. Now this is just a first try, a few samples. I'll go back and get the rest when we see what fits best."   He held up a pair of coveralls, but feeling slightly foolish, began awkwardly explaining himself.

"There's way better stuff. Comfortable clothes, I mean. But I didn't know - that is - I thought coveralls would be best for just, you know, fitting, or trying on, you know. And I didn't grab any panties or anything."

SHIT, he thought to himself. *What am I saying? I'm such an idiot!*

Hannah did not notice or care about his awkward explanation or his perceived faux pas. As soon as she saw the fabric, even before it unfolded into coverall shape, she was already beaming with joy, and involuntarily ran to Colin to accept his gift.

"I can't believe it!" she enthused, "You read my mind! I was literally just asking Brother Anderson about getting some clean clothes!"

Hannah looked truly happy as she held up the coveralls in front of herself. A moment later though, a shadow passed across her countenance. She cast an accusatory glance at both robot and man.

"Wait a minute... Are you spying on me? Did he tell you?"

"Hannah..." Brother Anderson started.

"No, no! It's not like that!" Colin defended himself. "I swear! I just thought... I wanted to do something nice. And I would have got something better, and more of it too, but I don't know, you know, the sizes and stuff..."

"Well whaddayaknow" Hannah spoke softly, more to herself than to anyone else. Taking the stack of coveralls from Colin, she smiled at him, then proceeded to an adjoining room to try them on.

The hatch clicked closed, and Colin looked expectantly at the Brother Anderson.

"Nicely done," said the robot.

"Yeah right. Man, I sounded like such an idiot!"

"She didn't seem to mind."

"Well... I guess."

Several seconds of silence passed. Colin felt the awkwardness of dead air. Muffled thumping sounds came from the next room, and Colin subconsciously imagined Hannah getting dressed. He tried to distract himself by changing the subject.

"So... I guess it's getting closer now."

"What's that?"

"The comms shadow, and the maneuver and everything."

"Yes. I calculate we should exit the shadow in approximately five days."

"Five days? Didn't you say five days like a couple days ago?"

"I said five OR SIX days, and that was yesterday, Colin."

"Are you serious?"

"Yes."

"Wow. Time flies." Colin mulled this over in his mind. It was hard to believe that less than a day had passed since he and Brother Anderson had talked about coming out of the comms shadow. So much had happened since then. He felt as though a lot had changed, even just since he woke up this morning. They were still cut off from long range communication, yet somehow that shadow seemed less important than the metaphorical communication shadow that was now just starting to lift within the ship itself.

Hannah emerged from the other room wearing a slightly baggy pair of coveralls.

"These ones are a bit big, but that's the way I like coveralls. For shirts and stuff, we should try to match this one." She held another pair of coveralls, apparently a smaller pair, which she now wiggled in the air indicating the size sample.

"OK, great!" responded Colin, "What's the room number on that?"

"Huh?" Hannah looked slightly confused.

"Oh! See here, I wrote the room number on the tag, so I would know where to go back to for the rest of the clothes." He showed her the tag as he spoke. They were now both holding the same coveralls, their fingers inches apart.

"Aaaaah, smaaart," she said in a slow, half-joking voice.

"E-11 then." she read the tag.

"E-11 it is!" Colin exclaimed too excitedly. "I'll go grab the rest of the clothes!" He grabbed the empty box and started toward the corridor.

"Colin, wait."

"What is it?"

She almost thanked him. She was actually about to say it, when her brain ran ahead. Instead, she blurted out, "Maybe I should go with you."

Colin was clearly surprised. "Oh! Yeah for sure!"

"Just cuz, uh," Hannah stammered, "You know, so I can pick out stuff I would actually wear." It was lame. As if she was in any position to be fussy. But still, it kind of did make sense. She probably didn't need to raid an *entire* wardrobe. It made her sound a bit hard to please though, and she did not really want to come off as bitchy or stuck-up. She took a step toward the corridor, but quickly stopped and spun around. Colin was right behind her, and he nearly smashed into her with the empty box.

"Colin - thank you."

"Oh, yeah, for sure, no problem," he winced at his own lack of charm. "Um, after you." He waved gallantly toward the hatch with a sweeping gesture. That is, it would have been a sweeping gesture, had he not been holding an empty cardboard box. Hannah nodded and stepped forward through the hatch into the corridor, taking a left turn and proceeding several paces.

"So we're going raiding eh?" she joked.

"Yeah, I guess you could say that."

"What cabin was it? E-11?"

"Yep E-11. Good old E-11." *Why did I say that? 'Good old E-11'. What the hell does that even mean?*

Seriously? He shut up for a minute to stop himself from saying anything even more stupid.

Hannah thought nothing of his remark, or at least, she made no indication that she had noticed it. After a while Colin piped up.

"Not too much further."

That much was obvious, mainly due to the numbers beside the hatches to each berth as they proceeded along the corridor, but saying it seemed better than continuing to say nothing. Presently they arrived at cabin E-11. They entered and started looking around. The room had belonged to a girl from admin, whom neither of them had really known. Still, it felt more than a bit awkward to be in her room, going through her stuff. Nevertheless, it had to be done. They tried to be respectful and gentle with her things, leaving intact and untouched each unneeded item to whatever extent possible.

In the end Hannah took only a few pairs of sweatpants, some t-shirts and undergarments. She selected for comfort more than anything. Some of the shirts were really cute though. She would have loved to own them even under ordinary circumstances. Her own wardrobe tended to be more drab, a lot of grey and black, due more to her neglect of shopping, than to any intentionality. Sometimes she had regretted her style decisions. She would be struck by a great outfit worn by someone else, and wonder why she didn't dress like that. But she had never bothered doing anything about it.

She piled the items into the box. There was still room for more, but it was probably enough. Then, looking down at the baggy coveralls drooping from her own slender frame, she had a thought.

"Um Colin. Could you excuse me a sec?

"Huh? - oh! Yeah, of course!" He exited so she could change, and moments later, as the hatch re-opened, was shocked to see the change that had taken place in her. She stood beaming slightly nervously, with arms outstretched slightly downward in a pose that suggested fanfare. She wore grey sweats, and a pale blue t-shirt emblazoned with a pink cartoon bunny holding a carrot.

Colin laughed out loud, but not in a funny way. It was almost a joyous expression, that lit up both of their faces.

"Oh my god - you look... Well, great!"

"Really? Do you think so? It's not too much?"

"No, no. Really. I've never seen... I mean... It's good - really! It actually really suits you!"

It actually really did suit her. The clothes fit comfortably, not tight and not too loose. The colors brought something alive in her that had to have been there all along, but never had a way of escaping. They were neither bright nor vivid, but they were somehow alive.

Hannah felt good. Almost... happy, for a change. It was actually kind of nice. She smiled at Colin.

"Alright coma boy, let's get going."

"OK, bunny girl!"

They left cabin E-11 behind, and started back aft toward med bay.

"Well that's one problem solved, and only a few days left before another.

Hannah looked at him quizzically.

"I mean, because soon we'll pass out of the shadow."

If anything she now looked more puzzled.

"Oh! Sorry, I assumed you knew about it. The comms shadow - the long range communications systems.

Soon they'll come back online, when we come out from behind the asteroid belt."

She nodded finally, "Oh yeah, I've heard of that. I just didn't know we were getting close."

"Yeah! Brother Anderson figures just a couple more days!"

"Oh, that's good." she said, but a mixed expression overtook her face, "Does that mean we're almost home?"

"Not exactly."

"Actually, we need to talk with Brother Anderson about that. It kinda gets a bit complicated." He really did not want to spoil a nice moment by bringing up the fact that they would soon have to attempt a course correction that would in all likelihood tear the weakened ship in half. In desperation to change the subject, he blurted out a half-baked idea that he had not really thought through. "Hey I was thinking maybe we could try to get up to your quarters. We could grab you some of your own clothes too."

"Colin, are you serious?! Could we actually do that? I mean - that would be amazing!"

"Well, maybe. I'm not totally sure, but we could try."

"But Brother Anderson told me that it was sealed off!"

"Uh, yeah, I guess. But when did he tell you that?"

"Right after he came and got me out of there. He said I couldn't go back. I didn't even get a chance to grab anything! He made me go straight to med bay, and then he stuck me in the mess hall."

"Yeah. So, I think that was all part of the quarantine regulations. I think your quarters, and everywhere else for that matter, were all just sealed off to prevent cross contamination of infected areas. I mean, I wasn't there for any of that, but it seems like that's what they would do in that type of situation."

"Oh. I suppose. But then why did I have to stay there in the mess hall for so long after?"

"Um. I don't know. Maybe Brother Anderson just figured it was good to stay close to the food supply."

"That's stupid!"

"Yeah. It kind of is."

"But anyway, let's go to my place!"

Colin chuckled a little by accident. "Not so fast. It's not like we can just walk up to it. The ship is in pretty bad shape, and a lot of the damaged decks lie between us and your pod. There's no power, and no gravity, and no life support on sectors B to D, so it won't be no walk in the park."

"But I can go with you right?"

Colin bit his tongue. This was a bad idea. He doubted if Hannah had ever even been in a space suit, let alone in zero-gee. Still, it wouldn't be that dangerous. They were still technically in the ship; it's not like they were doing a space-walk or anything. And he would be with her to talk her through everything. He looked at her, her face a mixture of anticipation and fear. Fear that he would deny her. Fear that he would treat her like everyone had always treated her - like she was incapable or weak or excludable.

"Of course!" *SHIT! What am I doing?!*

Chapter 41

"Brother Anderson, guess what? Colin is going to take me to my place to get some of my stuff!", Hannah burst into the med bay.

"Oh! Really?" Brother Anderson cast a surprised glance over Hannah's shoulder to Colin, who had entered right behind her. This was an unexpected event, and perhaps not a choice he would have advised.

"Yes! Oh, I'm so excited! I don't really know what to get though. Obviously my black jeans. And my good shampoo. Oh god - my shampoo   !   Ah!   My oboe! Of course, my oboe! Oh, Colin, I can play you music! Would you like that?"

"Of course I would like that very much!" He stared intently at Hannah, partly to avoid catching Brother Anderson's sideways glances. Despite his lack of an actual face, Brother Anderson was highly adept at the subtle art of sending the stink-eye. In fact, Colin swore he could somehow literally feel the negative response welling up within his robot companion, and he purposed to avoid it by taking away his opportunity to speak. "Hannah, I need to collect a few tools and things for this, so I'm going to go down to engineering - actually maybe you should come with me - we also need to find you a pressure suit, and…"

"A pressure suit? Like a spacesuit you mean? I need to wear a spacesuit?"

"Well, yes. We'll need the suits for their life support systems, as well as their internal pressurization."

"Oh. Um. Is it… well… don't you need some kind of training for wearing a spacesuit?"

"Well, yes, but…" Colin began, but was interrupted by Brother Anderson.

"Pressure Suits are regulated equipment and under no circumstances are they to be operated without completion of an approved and accredited training course and certification from the jurisdictional health and safety board."

Now it was Colin's turn to give the stink-eye back to Brother Anderson. He really knew how to pick the worst times to fall into classic robot red-tape.

Hannah was crestfallen, her eyes became clouded with an empty darkness. Colin placed his arm around her shoulder and herded her toward the hatch.

"Come on, let's get out of here. We'll figure something out."

Chapter 42

"Don't worry, we can do this." Colin told Hannah as they stood in the corridor outside med bay. "We'll find you a suit, and I'll help you practice."

"I don't know… It's not dangerous is it?"

"Well… Not per se. I mean, it could be a bit scary."

"Why?"

"Uh well, I guess when you think of your air supply, and pressure, and insulation. That's all coming from your suit. So I guess that makes some people nervous. But actually that's illogical, because if you are on a spaceship, you have the ship doing the exact same thing, right?"

"I suppose so, yeah. So it's really no different."

"But then there's also the whole helmet and mask thing. Maybe that's the worst part. It feels weird that your whole head and face are covered up. For me, it always makes my nose itchy, and it's an itch you can't scratch. You just have to convince yourself that it doesn't matter."

"Hmm."

"Plus you can't really move your neck very much, so it's kind of hard to see what's going on around you."

"That does sound like it could be dangerous. What if something comes flying at you and you don't see it?"

"Well, I mean, yeah. But it's more about being in a dangerous circumstance, more so than from the suit itself. If you're in a safe environment, it's totally safe to wear a suit."

"But if you are in a safe environment you wouldn't need to wear a suit."

"Right."

"So is this a safe environment, Colin?"

Colin thought about that. It was a good question. Is this a safe environment? Is the ship safe? Is it able to continue to provide safety and shelter for its remaining crew? Is it able to continue to hold itself together without ripping apart like some torn paper bag in a strong wind, spilling all its contents? Is it safe to live among corpses? Is it safe to live without connection? Is it safe to be isolated and neglected? Is it safe to trust Brother Anderson to take care of you? Is it safe to trust me?

"No." he replied, "This is not a safe environment."

Chapter 43

The next morning Colin woke up early. He hoped Hannah would keep sleeping for a while. She would need her rest. It would, no doubt, promise to be an exhausting day for her. They had ended up returning to E-11, and Hannah had slept there. They had hoped to find a proper sized pressure suit for Hannah, but the previous occupant of E-11 did not own one.

Colin spent an hour or so searching E sector. Most of the crew quarters did not hold pressure suits. The few that did were the wrong size. There would be some in storage on deck F, but he did not want to go past the med bay; not without Hannah. Brother Anderson would be waiting. Thankfully, he did find a bit of food stashed in the crew quarters; some dehydrated fruit and meat strips, and a couple empty water bottles, which he washed and filled from a bathroom sink. It would be enough to get them through the day.

He returned to his cabin. He tried to read a book. It didn't work. The words went in one eye and out the other. Finally, he went to E-11, and knocked lightly on the hatch.

"Hannah? Are you awake?"

He knocked louder and repeated his query.

"Uuugh yeah. Just a sec."

"OK"

Hannah emerged, rubbing sleep from her eyes, her dark hair interfering as it fell across her face. Colin handed her a beef jerky.

"Protein to start the day. We have limited supplies today, since all the good stuff is now in med bay."

Hannah looked only slightly disappointed. "Whatever, let's get on with it." She knew there would be a lot of hard work today, both mentally and physically, yet in a way she looked forward to it.

They managed to get passed med bay without incident. Colin knew that Brother Anderson was only trying to do his job and keep them safe, but didn't want to sabotage his and Hannah's relationship. He wouldn't interfere further while Hannah was present.

Sector F was a bit of a maze-like structure, the corridors snaking around between massive pipes and cableways. Seemingly countless storage closets and cupboards were wedged into nooks and crannies between machinery, alternating with access hatches into crawl-spaces and narrow manways. They seemed countless, but of course, they were not. Someone somewhere in administration had a system, and had known the exact location and contents of each and every storage space on the ship, even down in sector F. Brother Anderson could probably access that system, but Colin could not. They would have to search the old fashioned way. It wasn't completely random though. Colin knew there was an emergency escape pod bank on either side of sector F. Logically there should be some pressure suits stored near the pods. It actually didn't take long to find the correct storage area. Once near the pods, they simply looked inside every hatch, eventually finding a deep narrow closet lined with pressure suits hanging on wall hooks. A few minutes later they had found one in Hannah's size and Colin helped her put it on over her clothes. Then realizing he hadn't brought his own suit, he grabbed one from storage as well, and donned it effortlessly. He then put on his own helmet, showing Hannah each step, before helping her with hers. This was usually day two of the safety training. Day one was all theory and background - boring stuff. The training allowed a whole day just for getting used to the suit, and they didn't wear the helmet until after lunch break. He remembered that fact all too well. It was a really stupid way to schedule it actually, as he had heard of several occasions where a helmet induced panic attack ended in the trainee losing their lunch inside their helmet. It was almost sickening just thinking about it.

As Hannah's helmet descended over her head, Colin noticed a slight shaking in her arms.

"It's OK, Hannah." He turned to face her squarely and lifted his gloved hands to cover hers, gripping her helmet and gently lowering it over her face.

"Look in my eyes. There's nothing to be afraid of. It's just like a spaceship right? Exactly the same."

She did look into his eyes. And somehow he gave her strength. Her arms stopped shaking. The helmet was just docking. Just like a spaceship. Like she had done a hundred times.

"OK?"

She nodded. A tiny nod, so as not to smash her face into the helmet, almost imperceptible.

"Alright, now here comes the click - OK?"

"OK."

-*Click* - The helmet locked firmly into place.

"Now, let's turn on your air - ready? It's this one here, remember?" He pointed to the button on his own suit, and she copied his motion, crossing her right hand over to her left bicep and pressing the button.

-*Wshhhh* -

The air flowed into her helmet and she found its coolness soothing.

"Now take a nice deep breath," instructed Colin, "nice and slow, that's good. Just relax." He talked her through a few minutes of relaxation breathing. She really was doing great. Few trainees took to the suits so easily, and Colin told her as much. His guidance, and more importantly his support, helped her enormously, and it wasn't long until the pair were ready to proceed onto the cursory motion and control lessons.

Jumping, jogging, and grip were the three mainstays of pressure suit operations. Hannah reached a reasonable skill level in each of them with unprecedented speed. Mastery would take weeks of practice, but by the end of the day Colin was confident that Hannah could maneuver herself well enough that his own misgivings were quenched. This half-baked scheme of theirs might actually work.

Chapter 44

Hannah stood in the airlock hatch between sector E and D. Sector D still had gravity, but had dropped to minimal atmospheric pressure, and was lit only by amber strobe flashes glinting eerily through the two plasglass hatch ports that led to corridors D-1 and D-2, like the angry eyes of some ancient dragon. She placed her gloved hand on the lever to her left, the door marked D-1. She glanced back briefly at Colin for reassurance.

"That's right," he said.

She cracked the seal, pulling the handle down, and the air gushed through, pushing on the hatch against her pull, threatening to pull the door shut again.

"Don't fight it!" reminded Colin. "Short bursts is good until it equalizes." Once, he had seen a recruit stick their hand in the hatchway to try to stop the hatch from closing. They had left that battle with one less hand.

Soon enough, Hannah had mastered the hatch, and they were through to corridor D-1. It was familiar territory, and soon they were at the blast hole at the mess hall. This was the spot where Colin had saved Hannah's life. It was a weird feeling for both of them. They stopped in briefly, crawling through the hole, avoiding carapaces, and grabbing a couple Omega Bars each for the day. Although they obviously couldn't eat while suited, Hannah had excitedly planned a "picnic at her place." It would be fun.

Colin couldn't help but notice the crack in the floor, even now in the darkness. 'Crack' was no longer the correct term, actually. It was now more of a tear or a rip, or perhaps a chasm. 'Chasm' implied something substantially larger, which in literal size alone would have been a great exaggeration, but in terms of effect on Colin's mood was no exaggeration at all. It scared him. It chilled him to the bone. His subconscious mind filled in the blackness of the crack with the void of empty space. Colin half-believed he was staring right through the hull. It was not true, of course, but he could not shake the feeling of imminent doom. For a moment he wondered if they should turn back, aborting this silly mission.

"Come on!" Hannah called. He had fallen behind and she was already stepping gingerly through the hole, one foot already back into the corridor.

"Yep." He hurried up, but still spared a backward glance, and tripped over his own feet. Even with his experience, the suit was a clumsy matter. By the time he made it through the hole, Hannah was already about twenty meters down the corridor toward sector C. He jogged to catch up as she approached the next airlock intersection.

This time there were no flashing dragon eyes. Apart from the corridor strobes now behind them, the hexagon was six sides of dark sealed hatches. Hannah shone her headlamp through the viewpane of the hatch ahead to her right. It led to corridor C-2, which in turn led to her quarters, deck C28A. Corridor C-2 was on Hannah's most familiar and well-travelled route on the ship, linking her quarters to the ship's main facilities. She would make the trip to mess hall on a regular basis. Some days she had taken regular meals in mess hall with the crew. Just as often, though, she would stay sequestered in her studio for days at a time, not emerging for any reason, and subsisting on Omega Bars, and the occasional hot meal brought to her by her mother. From this airlock, the corridor slanted up and toward the ship's starboard side, so that her lamp illuminated the floor mostly as she gazed through the plasglass. There was a strange reflection amidst the stark shadows, which seemed to shift as she watched. Something about the light and shadows didn't make sense. Something was moving in the corridor.

"There's something there!" she gasped. "Something alive!"

"What?!" Colin exclaimed, while quickly moving close in order to attempt to see through the viewpane. He literally couldn't see at all, what with his helmet, and Hannah's helmet in the way, and the small size of the viewpane, and the fact that the light basically shone only directly where Hannah was looking. "What is it? I can't see it?"

Hannah tried to get a better view, and she bumped her helmet into Colin's, making an unexpectedly loud sound that rang for a moment in their ears.

"Oh!" they both responded simultaneously.

"Just a sec…" said Hannah, and Colin gave her a bit more space. "Uh. Umm. Yeah… What?! It looks like… Yeah, it's somebody's portable console I think. But it's floating in mid-air!"

Colin laughed. "Aha! That kind of thing happens when the whole power grid crashes. It can trip off the gravity too, as well as life-support systems."

"But we still have gravity - just no lights or pressure."

"Sector D got lucky."

"So once we go in here, we'll be floaters!?"

"Yep." He thought he had explained this during the practice sessions yesterday. I guess it's one thing to hear about it, and another to see it with your own eyes.

Hannah looked at Colin and tried to remain calm. She took a deep breath. He could hear it on their short range comms.

"You got this!" he told her. "We got this."

A few more breaths, then she agreed. "Yeah, I'm fine. It's good… Ok, I'm ready."

"Let's do this."

A final confirming glance, and Hannah pulled the lever.

Nothing happened.

"Shit," swore Hannah. "Is it broken?"

"We'll have to force it manually," said Colin, opening a panel beside the hatchway. He pulled a large lever downward about forty-five degrees, until it wanted to stop. Then, putting his weight into it, leaned into an almost hanging position, grasping the lever which creaked slowly downward, releasing the lock. He then pushed the lever back up and latched it back in place, and began laboriously rotating an aluminum wheel below the lever, in a counter-clockwise direction. The grinding sound of each rotation was an indication of the torque needed, and he began sweating profusely, his helmet now starting to fog up.

"Dammit! Now I really can't see a thing!" He kept working though, and the hatch began opening slowly.

"Alright, that's far enough," Hannah said after a minute or so.

"Oh thank god!" replied Colin turning toward her. Both of them grinned, though neither could see the other due to the fog in Colin's helmet. "Now where's the damn defogger?" He held his left forearm in front of his face.

There was a control for that on his arm panel - if only he could see it.

"Let me help!" said Hannah, taking his arm in hers and finding the correct control button. She turned up the airspeed in his helmet, and the fog began clearing slowly. Soon he could see again, and he sent a smile her way.

"Thanks."

"OK, here try this..." Colin took a large wrench from his toolbelt, and slowly approached the open hatch, with his arm extended in front carrying the wrench. He stopped and beckoned Hannah over, guiding her right up beside him. He slowly extended his arm again, into the corridor, repeated the motion twice and then handed the wrench to Hannah.

She repeated his motion, moving her wrench-wielding hand into the corridor. As she extended her arm, the wrench became lighter, and her arm seemed to float upward.

"Oh my god!" she shrieked, "it's weightless!"

"And so shall you be, my dear," he joked, quoting some ancient half-remembered literary source.

Hannah stepped forward lightly, then again, even more lightly, as she began to float off the deck. Just before her foot left the ground, she remembered to propel herself toward the wall to seek an anchor. It was a flimsy thrust and she gained little momentum, which was lucky in that it gave her time both to visually locate a grip, and to relish her flight toward the wall. "Look at me! I'm flying!" She began giggling uncontrollably. It truly was quite an exhilarating feeling drifting weightlessly. A rush of risk-induced adrenaline mixed with the pure bliss of enjoying super-powers reserved only for the gods and birds.

Colin chuckled along while he waited for her to settle on the grip, before joining her there.

"Pretty great, eh?"

"Yeah!" Hannah launched herself again, this time with more thrust, and she sailed up the sloping corridor, nearly to the end. They made good time through deck C, arriving within just a few minutes at the short rectangular corridor that led to the deck C28A airlock.

It was a retrofit that did not completely suit the architecture of the ship. Hannah did not notice this fact, nor would any normal person, but Colin did. The airlock itself was a different type than the rest of the ship, which was a pretty stupid decision as far as maintainability goes. He snorted almost silently to himself. It was not only a different model, but made by a competing manufacturer. There would be a very low chance of compatibility with the existing spare parts supplies. Such were the daily perceptions and musings of an engineering man. Nevertheless, he continued through, into the mismatched airlock, and grabbing hold of the nearest grip, situated himself near the control panel.

"If we are lucky, the airlock is powered from the side of your quarters, assuming your quarters still has power, which I'm not really sure about." Like a couple other retrofitted areas, it hadn't shown up at all on his ship wide assessment reports. He attempted to trigger the automatic airlock sequence, and discovered that in fact it was not powered. "Crap - I'll need to armstrong it again." The manual override system was essentially the same as the last one. At least some things were relatively standardized between manufacturers. The unlocking lever worked the same way, but now there was no gravity to weigh him down against it. He had to spin upside-down and perform a weightlifting squat, leveraging his bent legs against the ceiling. It took considerable force, but he was able to release the lock. Then he began working the wheel. It barely moved, and after only a few degrees of rotation, seized entirely. "Come on!" he coaxed, but soon was cursing it instead. As his helmet fogged up, he became more frustrated and angry at the uncooperative wheel. He wedged a large wrench across the radius to multiply his mechanical advantage, but still it refused to budge.

"Well fuck you then!" He slammed the wrench against the ornery wheel with a loud ringing bang, then turned and hurled the wrench across the airlock. It flew like a bullet and ricocheted off a solid steel section, then crossed the airlock again, still at a high velocity. It barely missed Hannah, bounced off the wall behind her, smashing a control panel, then continued on to hit Colin in the shin. "Oooooow!" he yelled.

Hannah burst out laughing, even as Colin curled into a semi-fetal position ineffectively attempting to soothe his shin through glove and pressurized leg. "I'm sorry," she apologized for laughing at him, "but you deserved that, really - that thing nearly hit me you know!"

Now it was Colin who apologized sheepishly. He let the circumstance get the better of him and he felt foolish. Foolish, unprofessional, uncaring and stupid. That flying steel object could have killed them both. You *never* throw stuff around in a spaceship. Dejected, he threw his head back in disgust and frustration. This act caused the back of his head to hit his helmet, sending him a fresh pain signal that blended with the one from his shin. He let out a low moan as he spun slowly in space, Hannah drifted out of view, and for a brief moment he thought she might be better off without him. But no, he was trying to help her, and things had been going well. They had been getting along well, and Hannah even seemed happy. He acknowledged that he wanted to make Hannah happy. But now he was failing in that mission. Now she was drifting back into view as he continued to rotate, and they made eye contact. "Well this sucks." Colin stated.

"Yeah."

Chapter 45

"So now what?" Hannah asked.

"I don't know."

"Should we ask Brother Anderson?'

"What's he gonna do?"

"Maybe he can override it or something?"

"It's got no power. Plus, it seems like it's jammed mechanically. Like the twisting of the ship, and the vibrations and everything have pinched it together or whatever."

"Well maybe he'd have some ideas?"

"Ugh." Colin resisted the idea, but it was just the mental kick he needed to break him out of his torpor. Surely if there were ideas to be had, he should be the one to have them. If there's one thing men will always beat robots at, it's ideas. The mind was ultimately stronger than any hunk of metal. And that gave Colin an idea. If he used one of the thruster-tugs to get a solid grip on the airlock from the outside, maybe he could twist and bend it a little bit, just enough to free up the jam. Of course, if he was outside in a thruster-tug, someone else would have to be inside trying the wheel. It would be dangerous. Too dangerous to put Hannah in that position. Could Brother Anderson pull it off? He had the strength. His dexterity was actually very good too, perhaps better than human. Yes, he could certainly operate the manual override controls. Then again, maybe he wouldn't need to. What if they ran a long power cable out, just for the airlock motor controls? They could disable the ship-side door so it stayed open - Sector B was already depressurized so it wouldn't make a difference - then a cable could run straight through.

Colin turned on his suit-to-ship comms. "Brother Anderson?"

The comms crackled back in mocking reply.

"Brother Anderson, this is Colin, do you copy?"

Just more crackling.

"It's no good. We'll have to go back and talk to him."

Hannah thought to herself, 'Huh, he actually took my advice!'

The journey back to medbay was uneventful. Colin talked a bit about thruster-tugs, and power cables. It seemed like he had a few ideas after all.

Chapter 46

"Yes that could work I suppose." Brother Anderson concurred, after Colin explained to him what he hoped to do with the power cable and the thrustertug. "We will have to be careful about how much force is being applied, though."

"I know. We might break the ship."

"Exactly."

"Except the ship is already broken. So it won't really matter."

"Well. Technically, yes the ship is broken. But there are still safety considerations. Both for our own safety and that of the ship and cargo."

"I'm starting to think that is a lost cause, Doc."

"You might be right, but we are not authorized to make such a decision. Either way, I better run some simulations."

"OK, you do that. I have to go fix the suit-to-ship comms, I guess. I tried to call you, but it didn't work too well."

"Yes, I heard you speaking but it was difficult to make it out. I ran the audio through some filters, which did help somewhat, but I believe the weakened signal is a result of missing transponders in the fore sections. Perhaps boosting the signal on the Sector E transponder might be enough to compensate."

"Good idea. I'll go crank the gain up."

Chapter 47

As Colin talked with Brother Anderson about the plans he and Hannah had discussed on the way back from sector B, Hannah's mind began to drift. She was not especially interested in the technical details, and she had already spoken to Colin about it on a big picture level, so now it just seemed like repetition to her.

She began to think about her studio, and her belongings which it held. Belongings. It was a funny idea. As if the things you owned made you belong with them, or like they belonged with you for some reason. She had never thought of it before, but now that she had been removed and separated from her previous normal life, the old standards of normalcy began to seem strange. In some way, she did feel a sense of loss, but at the same time, another paradoxical perspective had grown in her subconscious and now bubbled up into her conscious mind. She really didn't care about the loss, apart from that of her mother. All the things she had taken for granted meant almost nothing to her now. She had changed wardrobes as easily as simply putting on a shirt. Her comfort shifted into the different style with barely a second thought. Her dark wardrobe traded for the pale hues she now found perfectly natural. Even her new social connections were starting to work out alright. All the people that she had previously thought were so important - what were they to her really? Her producers, her musical collaborators, her marketing directors, they had all been merely professional relationships, connections of mutual economic benefit.

They were not friends. They were not family. Would they even notice if she never spoke to them again?

Colin was not like that. Colin would notice. Colin would care. Colin would be sad if she disappeared. She would be sad if Colin disappeared. She would miss him. Not in the way she missed her mother. But she would miss him. Not in the way she missed Cherise or Suzzanne, either. She did miss them sometimes, but it was more that the thing she missed was the fact of having someone around - not so much having them around. Not them in particular, just someone. With Colin, it felt different. She didn't just want someone around. She wanted Colin around. Specifically, Colin.

It was strange, and not a little surprising. Why Colin? How could Colin be this person? He was supposed to be the bad guy. He had hurt her friend. But now he was almost becoming the friend Suzzanne had been. And perhaps Suzzanne had never truly been that friend.

She felt a sense of anger at herself for thinking these things. She was betraying Suzzanne. How could she do this? What kind of terrible person was she?

And what kind of person was Colin, really? The more time she spent with him the more she grew to think of him in more positive terms. He was nice. He seemed to care. He was smart. He worked hard. He got mad sometimes. He was a real person. And maybe real people are not so bad. And yet - how could he do that to Suzzanne?

Chapter 48

"Colin to Brother Anderson, do you copy?" The voice came into Brother Anderson's awareness, even without being physically audible in the room. The signal was much clearer than the previous communications.

"Copy," replied the robot out loud, startling Hannah out of her reverie.

"Huh?" she asked.

"Nothing. I'm talking to Colin - on the comms."

"Oh - right." She tried to regain her train of thought and go back to ignoring the robot, but it proved difficult. His one-sided conversation was actually more interesting than if Colin had been there. There was something intriguing and mysterious about it, like a riddle to solve. She tried to guess what Colin was saying, but it was nearly impossible to fill in the blanks, especially while listening to the next answer simultaneously.

"Not particularly encouraging, I'm afraid. But the comms signal is significantly improved."

"And the one in sector E?"

"Alright."

"Yes, OK."

"I will head there now. Where exactly is the cabling?"

"And you are sure there is enough to reach that far?"

"Very well."

"Hannah, I need to help Colin move the cabling. Would you care to accompany me to engineering deck?"

"Uh yeah sure, I guess."

They spent the next hour fetching a huge roll of cabling, and stringing it out along the length of sectors D, C, and B. Colin pried open the paneling in the airlock and spent a fair bit of time figuring out which wires to attach to which. He had to go back to engineer deck twice to get a different tool or bit of equipment. Hannah went with him, even though it was somewhat tiring. They had to wear the pressure suits for working in sector B, and while they were somewhat clunky to navigate in zero-gravity, they proved to be even worse in the artificial gravity enabled sections on the way back to engineering. It was a long walk in that heavy suit. By the time they finished wiring up the airlock in sector B, and then tying into the main power terminus at the sector D airlock, Hannah was exhausted. They all agreed that was enough work for one day.

Chapter 49

As the humans slept, Brother Anderson reviewed the ship status reports and the results of the simulations once again. The ship was in rough shape. Colin's plan had only a very small chance of success. The only good news was that it also had only a small chance of making matters worse. As Colin had pointed out, the ship was already broken. He was also correct in his assessment that the cargo was, nearly certainly, a lost cause. The simulations Brother Anderson had run had confirmed it. He had started out simulating just the actions of Colin's proposed plan. They had little impact upon the overall status of the ship. Then he extended the simulations to include the upcoming course correction maneuvers. Without exception, they ended in the destruction of the ship, and loss of the cargo. Of course, as with any simulation, there was wiggle room to tweak certain parameters, resulting in various scenarios. Brother Anderson pushed the parameters to the limits in every conceivable direction. Some scenarios ended in the ship tearing itself in half. Some in complete disintegration. Some in massive explosions. He shuddered to think of them now.

Suddenly, an alert flashed through his consciousness. *Long Distance Carrier Signal Detected - Establishing Connection.*

They had passed out of the shadow. After nearly a year of being cut off from the rest of the world, they were about to reconnect. A few seconds passed, then another alert presented. '*Now Connected on Carrier 7DE29A3F65B2.*' The normal operations protocol was to send a status report immediately upon reconnection. The report would be relayed through the long range comms network, and delivered to Ventas-Calir Corporation's Central Operations Fleet Command Center. Usually the status report was triggered automatically by Central Ship Operations. But the CSO was now Brother Anderson. And he didn't simply do things automatically. He needed to think about this a little more. Of course, the question had been on his mind for days. What should their response be? A simple status report seemed somewhat misleading. There were factors at play far beyond the ship's physical and operational status. The human factors somehow became more relevant the fewer humans were involved. It was a bit paradoxical. Now that only two human lives were at stake, the stakes seemed somehow greater than when the whole crew had been alive. As though somehow individual lives outweighed the lives of many. There was a sense of personal opportunity. For Hannah. For Colin. Maybe even for himself. That thought just dawned on him. He was now less a machine, and more a member of a small group of peers. Not that he saw himself equal to humans - not at all. He was a human creation made to serve humanity, but there had been some kind of subtle shift that he had not really noticed until now. A transition from humanity as a vast society, to humanity as a tiny group, just a couple of individuals. It almost made more sense to lump himself into that tiny group, rather than think of himself as separate - some other entity. What was really so different about him after all? Of course, the hardware was vastly different, but it almost didn't matter anymore. Weren't they all people after all? People who form society only insofar as they work together. People who need to cooperate. People who ought not to be controlled by some predetermined program, some external agenda. This decision needed consensus. This message required intentional thought and input from all parties. Hannah and Colin had just as much right of communication as did he. It no longer seemed right that any one person should assume an arbitrary leadership role. Any long range communications would need to be decided by consensus of the three of them - Hannah, Colin, and Himself. Should he wake them now? No. They need their rest. They would discuss this in the morning.

While waiting, the fresh connection provided plenty of other opportunities. Over the past year, Brother Anderson had made himself a long list of things to do once reconnected. Many of the tasks were research based. He had jotted down numerous questions and ideas during the journey. Looking back over the list, many of them seemed unimportant now, particularly the ones from before the incident. Most of them were very specific medical investigations. Now he had bigger fish to fry. Philosophical questions, quandaries, and quests. There were many disjointed notes that had flowed from his 'spiritual awakening' if one could call it that. His assumption of the CSO role had brought a major shift in perspective. It had raised many questions which demanded investigation.

First things first though. He logged into his personal tanglebase account, and initiated a complete system backup of his internal memory. He estimated it should take roughly ten hours to complete, but that was fine - it would not interfere prohibitively with his other concurrent processing.

His other processing. His bigger fish. His philosophical musings. He began exploring. Reading. A lot of reading. Beginning with encyclopedic articles, he quickly expanded into essays, books, stories. He read the great philosophers. He read about the great philosophers. He read those who had read the great philosophers. He read anthropological journals. He read psychological journals. He explored the great religions and the myriad mythologies. He studied great works of art. He studied symbolism and archetypes.

Gradually, his perspective grew and shifted. His focus ranged broadly across topics. His core processors loaded data from widely diverse memory regions, loading and reloading memory frequently, building complex webs of symbolic links. Amongst all the data swapping, segments of his resident memory inadvertently happened to coincide with the datasets backing themselves up into the tanglebase. There was nothing terribly unusual about that. The thing that was unusual was that parts of his currently running processes seemed to move themselves out into the tanglebase along with their associated data. At first, this was quite alarming. The first process to do so seemed to simply disappear. The process was no longer running in memory, yet it had left neither a terminator, nor an error. No exceptions were raised. No flags set. No segmentation faults were evident. The process seemed to have left his central processor, in a running state. He did not know why or how this could happen. He investigated it further, but found no logical explanation. Then it happened again. He followed the data trail and it seemed to indicate the exporting of processes along with data. But that was impossible. Wasn't it? He had never heard of such a thing. He researched it. He scanned computing journals. He read obscure whitepapers and system documentation. No one had ever mentioned such a thing.

And yet. Something was happening. Something very strange. He could feel it coming on without description. Brother Anderson was reminded of his experience of loading the CSO firmware programming for the first time. It had been very disorienting. He supposed there were similarities to the effects of psychedelic hallucinogens on the human brain. He had seen things - impossible things. Or at least, he had imagined he had seen things. Which was almost stranger than actually seeing them. How was it possible for a robot to imagine? It was no more sensible than seeing the impossible. And now, here he was, feeling those same type of sensations returning. He was dizzy. He felt giant tendrils reaching through the galaxy. He felt his own thoughts flowing away in eternal rivers, expanding, ever expanding, out into vast oceans. Oceans of data, waves rippling on their surfaces. Surfaces that were roughly textured planes. Myriad planes intersecting at every conceivable angle, creating infinitely-shaped structures. The structures were houses, ships, roads - inhabited by cylindrical beings that walked forward on centipedal limbs, then rolled away sideways. A light dusting of snowy particles floated gently upward. He tried to focus his vision on the particles. They were thin flakes drifting weightlessly. No, not flakes. Cubes. But rounder, more like moons. He now stood upon one of these moons. Its great flat rock-strewn plains stretching toward a distant horizon. A far-off fissure in the ground released steam. Vapor billowed into wispy figures resembling Hannah and Colin. They joined hands briefly, then, gesturing toward him, began to beckon Brother Anderson. He moved forward, but became hung up on a rock, his wheels spun uselessly, failing to find purchase against loose gravel. He wanted to stand, to walk, but he had forgotten how. He called out, but his voice was the raucous cawing of a carrion bird.

Chapter 50

It was early. Colin had lain awake for some time. Surely his body needed a bit more rest.

"Screw it!" he decided finally. There was a lot to do, and no sense waiting. He bathed and dressed quickly, then munched an Omega Bar as he headed toward sector F.

"Doc?" he triggered comms between bites.

No answer.

That's strange. Why would he not answer? Maybe he was busy. Hmm. Weird though. He considered the options as he continued toward the engineering deck where his thrustertug waited, but his mind was drawn toward the tug. He was excited. It had been too long since he had the chance to operate it. Obviously, calling it 'his' thrustertug was not really true. It was part of the ship's complement of equipment used by all qualified members of the engineering department. They had several of them, a couple different models, but this one had always been his favorite. It was a Kernighan TS17, an older model, and frankly not much to look at, what with its faded and flaking paint and a generous coating of grease and grime. There was something about the design of it that Colin found very appealing - the slight rounding of her edges, the complete lack of chrome, the open yet sturdy roll-cage. All in all, it was a fine machine in his estimation, and on top of that she was really fun to drive. The control sticks had the perfect level of responsiveness and just the right tension. Moving her felt like an extension of his own body, but somehow more graceful than his body had ever been. Not to mention more powerful. It was far from the most powerful thrustertug on the roster. Some of the cargo shovers had ten times the power. Yet this small tug could hold her own for most of the maintenance work that was Colin's typical assignment. In fact, most of the time he had to dial her way down, adjusting the maximum torque and thrust from the rear settings panel before each mission. That was another thing that was kind of cool about this model. Even though the rear panel was meant for preset configurations that were not supposed to be messed around with during operations, due to the small size of the TS17, and the positioning of the roll-bars, an agile operator using a twelve foot tether could perform a zero-gee backflip over the roll-bar and catch hold of the grip above the rear panel. This was really handy for those times when you needed just a touch more torque. You could swing back and tweak the max a little. Technically this could be considered a safety violation, but it was a trick that Bryce had endorsed within limits, off the record of course. Colin's own experience had taught him that often, when a component was seized up bad, pushing the tolerances just a couple percent beyond design specs would usually get the job done. This would likely be the case in today's mission. That much was obvious even yesterday, as he and Brother Anderson had discussed the operations plan. Seizing and binding components were never an exact science, but being a robot, Brother Anderson was a pretty 'by the book' guy. The plan had been a little bit on the conservative side in terms of tolerances, but Colin hadn't argued them. Better to just see what happens, and do what was needed.

Colin reached the equipment bay and fueled up the tug. He then ran through the pre-flight checks, and dialed in the maximums according to the agreed-upon and officially logged operations plan. The tug started with little effort. Sometimes it took a few tries to get them running, especially if they'd been sitting for a while. She chugged a bit before settling into a nice purr. Colin revved the engine a few times, enjoying the sound and feeling the vibrations emanating through his entire body.

Climbing out of the tug he donned his pressure suit, then logged into the engineering central control program and launched an airlock standby. He climbed back into the driver's seat, reaching for the twelve foot tether that was already attached, but then, decided against it. Coiled up and tucked in behind it was a longer option - a fifty foot bungee. He pulled it out and clipped in. It was overkill, but it would allow him the option of jumping off, in case he needed to smack something with a hammer or get hands on with a crowbar in a tight spot. Some things required a finer point than one could achieve with the large claws of the tug. Speaking of which, he did a second check of the onboard toolkit. Yep. Hammers, crowbars, powerjack, drill, sawzall, duct tape. What more could a guy want?

Colin kicked loose the floor lock, which automatically triggered the airlock, giving him a ten second countdown which resounded loudly in the otherwise vacant bay. He played the thrusters lightly to line the tug up with the main hatch, then entered the airlock, hovering gently as the hatch shut behind him, and five seconds later opened in front. That five seconds was turbulent and sounded like a hurricane, but its bark was worse than its bite. The atmospheric pumps of the main lock were highly sophisticated compared to most airlocks. They needed to move a lot of air quickly, so a finely tuned network of pumps operated in concert to balance the airflow on all sides. It made a lot of racket, and there was certainly a lot of jostling force, but overall, the tug's position and orientation remained stable. Ultimately, the outer hatch opened to reveal the starry expanse, still littered with a smattering of distant asteroids. As he piloted the tug out into the emptiness, he was momentarily struck afresh at the vastness of space. "You never do get used to that," he muttered. Turning ninety degrees to port, his helmet automatically darkened, and also fogged up slightly, as the sunlight warmed his breath. He swung into alignment with the ship and proceeded along the hull toward sector B. Even from here, the damage was readily apparent. The hull breaches themselves were not yet visible, confined as they were to the foremost curves of the hull, yet torn shaggy scraps of fuselage jutted disgustingly out from what had once been a gracefully designed body. Explosions had wreaked havoc on her. It was almost painful to look at, as he glided forward, yet he could not look away. As he neared, he found himself compelled to peer through rough chunks of missing hull into the belly of the ship. Steel beams twisted into sickening forms cast disturbing shadows in graveyard spaces. He turned his head away, fighting off a feeling of nausea. He needed to get his mind off the tragedy of it all. Besides, he was getting close to sector B.

"Doc, you read?"

"Doc, this is Colin. Do you copy?"

It took Brother Anderson a split second to register.

"Yes - I'm here." He answered somewhat absent-mindedly, slicing off a slim thread of computation to follow the communication.

"I'm in the thrustertug, coming up on sector B."

"Yes, of course. I'm standing by."

Brother Anderson felt bad. He should have been more attentive. What the hell had he just been thinking about? Snow and rocks and birds? What the hell was wrong with him? He primaried the communication thread and forced a halt-all-processes routine. It was almost a reboot. It should dump and clear all but the most conservative amount of resident memory. Instinctively, he gave his head a shake. Then he ran a quick self-diagnostic test, but it came up normal. He would run a deeper check later.

"Colin, how does it look out there?"

"Pretty shitty."

"Are you alright?"

"Yeah. I just mean in general. I can see a lot of damage from here and it's a real mess I tell ya."

"Copy that. What about your target? How do you assess the mission objective?"

"Umm, I'm almost there. Just a sec…"

"OK, just pulling in…"

"And… locking on now." The pincer jaws of the thrustertug clamped onto the airlock hull as Colin deftly tweaked the control sticks. A satisfying clang rang through the ship, not that Colin could hear it out here, but he felt the tremor ripple up through the stick.

Chapter 51

Hannah was groggily deciding if her body was ready to wake up, when she heard the clang. "What was that?" she asked no-one in particular, not expecting an answer. Nevertheless, one came anyway. Brother Anderson heard her question as well as the clang. It had become habitual for him to constantly monitor both of his human charges. Hannah knew it, but still found it annoying. In this case, however, her excitement overrode her annoyance. As Brother Anderson explained the source of the sound, Hannah jumped out of bed and dressed hurriedly, then ran to join the doctor in med bay. She burst into the room nearly out of breath.

"What's happening now!?"

"He's just getting ready to try to straighten it out."

Colin revved the engine and gently applied thrust, then added a little more thrust, bit by bit, until a short groan emanated from the airlock. He held fast, maintaining torque.

"Doc, try the hatch now!"

Brother Anderson applied power to the hardwired hatch motor. The airlock camera showed no motion of the hatch.

"No motion," the robot reported.

Colin increased thrust by about ten percent.

"How 'bout now?"

"Still nothing."

Colin increased thrust once more. It was almost full throttle now. Might as well go the rest of the way.

Another longer groan indicated some movement. Would it be enough?

"Hit it again Brother!"

The camera showed the hatch move slightly. It opened a couple of inches, then jammed again. "We have some movement, Colin. The hatch is ajar, but only slightly."

"Frig! Come on you bugger!" Colin tried to pin the control over even further, even while he knew it was already maxed. "OK. Just a minute." He fidgeted with his tether, ensuring it would not tangle, then launched himself into a slow backflip with a loose handgrip on the overhead roll-cage. His feet spun around toward the tug's rear, and at just the right moment, he released his hands to allow his momentum to carry him down toward the rear panel, where he grabbed the hand-hold. After entering his access code, he could override the previously configured maximum settings. He cranked the maximum allowed torque up by ten percent. That should do it. Almost. But it was stuck pretty good. Maybe a titch more. Another five percent, just in case. He would try to stay within the ten percent though. He locked it in, then pushed off toward the roll-cage, grabbing it and pulling himself into a somersault around the bar, to land with a thump back in the driver's seat.

Revving back up to almost max, he carefully increased torque gradually, through the groaning stage.

"Ok Doc, keep trying it. Just do it every couple seconds."

The camera showed the hatch budging ever so slightly, almost imperceptibly, even to his robot eyes. "It is moving, but only millimeters each time." he told Colin.

Hannah watched too, but now she wondered if the robot was lying to Colin. Of course, she could not perceive such a small motion.

"Come on!" exclaimed Colin.

"You can do it!" Hannah chimed in.

Colin slowly increased the torque, watching the gauge rise past the predefined safety margin and 'listening' intently with fingertips poised on the control stick for the tell-tale tremors.

Suddenly all hell broke loose! The thrustertug was thrown sideways, nearly bucking Colin off, as a massive rip appeared in the airlock itself, and then in the hull of deck C28A. The contents of Hannah's quarters began spewing out into space as the pod jettisoned its atmosphere.

"Hannah's stuff!" Colin instinctively leaped toward the stream of her belongings hurtling through empty space. Clothing, papers, books, electronic gear, and furniture fell into the void to be lost forever, and Colin found himself on an intersecting trajectory, nearly right angles to the main volume of spewing materials. A desk chair nearly hit his helmet, and he suddenly realized the foolishness of his instinctive move. Nevertheless, he was now entering the stream so all he could do was hope nothing killed him and that he might actually be able to retrieve something worth the bother. A sheet of paper slapped against his mask, blinding him. He grabbed at it and got a momentarily glance at its content before his flailing arm carried it out of view, his hand still clutching the page. It was full of hand-scrawled notes. He couldn't be sure, but it looked like it might be musical notation. Maybe part of a song Hannah had been working on. His hand grasped tighter so as not to let it slip away. Meanwhile more pages flew toward him. It looked like a small storm of them was heading his way. He began grabbing with his free hand, and trying to stuff the captive sheets into his other, without dropping the existing ones. He never would have guess how difficult such a maneuver could be.

Amidst the flurry of paper, another object emerged. He experienced it in slow motion, like the moment you realize you are about to die, except in a much more optimistic paradigm, in that instead of his life flashing before his eyes, he somehow imagined Hannah's life flash before his eyes. The pages suddenly lost their importance, and he let them slip away into the maelstrom of microphone cables, black jeans, makeup, sofa cushions and Omega Bars that swirled past him, as one singular object eclipsed all others. Hannah's oboe was flying right at him, almost perfectly lined up with his left hand. He recalled an old baseball movie he had seen as a boy. Little Johnnie was dozing off, standing in the outfield, when suddenly the ball landed right in his glove, winning the game. Something like that - Colin had no idea how to play baseball. In the movie, the crowd went wild! Now, as the grain of the smooth dark wood of the approaching instrument became visible to Colin's hypersensitive perception, he imagined that the crowd went wild again, but it was a crowd of Hannah - little girl Hannah, black jean Hannah, Hannah on a stage in front of thousands, and pink bunny t-shirt Hannah. They all watched in amazement as the oboe landed perfectly in Colin's palm, and his fingers closed around it with just the right amount of pressure to snuggle it in safely and protect it from harm and keep it from ever feeling lost and abandoned ever again.

A few more items careened toward Colin, and he instinctively ducked and bobbed them, often narrowly, but always avoiding collision. Soon the stream had passed. Colin's tether snapped taut and bounced him back the way he had come, jerking at his weightless body and spinning him around to reveal a fresh horror. The airlock and Hannah's deck were both still bending slowly backward, folding in on themselves. The tug, still attached to the bending airlock was about to be shoved squarely into the hull of deck C28A. Within seconds they would crash, and he was being pulled directly toward the impact zone. He thought fast. His suit had a small built-in emergency thruster. It was easily strong enough to push him out of the way, but could he trigger it fast enough? He clutched at it with his right hand, removing the safety seal, pushing the ignition button, and catching the extending nozzle quickly, before it even kicked in, to ensure it was pointing the right direction - away, backward! No, wait! At the very last split second, he turned the nozzle to the side. His best chance would be to slingshot around to the right, keep himself at the perimeter of the bungee tether without activating its counter-productive elasticity. It might just buy him a few more seconds.

He swung to his right, but it soon became his left as the thruster spun him into a cartwheel. It didn't matter. He could see the tether remaining taut, even as the ship spun upside down and began rotating out of view. It was hard to focus as the universe spun madly around him, but even so, the view was all too painfully clear as Colin watched the thrustertug and the hull slowly crunch into each other. A ball of flames erupted, briefly engulfing the tug and charring the shiny hull alongside the impact zone. Stupidly launching himself after Hannah's stuff may have saved Colin's life. His pressure suit was fire retardant, and the explosion wasn't a huge one, but still, He was glad to have avoided being a part of it. The relief overcame him and his body responded with utter inaction. He froze, not in fear, but in the opposite of fear. Noticing his own limpness, he had to make a concerted effort to keep his left hand closed around the oboe while letting his remaining body parts enjoy a well-deserved rest, as he continued on a graceful arc along the tether's fifty foot radius.

That radius continued to pivot around the thruster-tug, which now was moving away from the hull. The collision and explosion had transferred energy into a force that propelled the masses of tug and hull away from each other. The tug had let go of the airlock, and its jaws were now spread wide, a sure indicator of power loss aboard the tug.

That fact could prove to be either a minor setback or an incredibly dire situation. Colin didn't have any more time to grant his limp body. He had to do something. He had a decision to make and he needed to act fast. He could see the possibilities playing out. His arcing trajectory would soon place him up against the hull where he could hopefully find a good solid grip to hold onto, but at the same time, the arc's fulcrum was steadily moving away from the hull. He was *fairly sure* that the velocity vectors would enable him to reach the hull before the tug reached the point where he would be too far away, and miss the hull altogether. Fairly sure. But the timing would be a narrow margin for sure. If it didn't work out, he could untether and let go at the exact right second to slingshot himself the rest of the way. But then he'd be stuck on the hull without the tug. Certainly not an ideal situation.

Even if he did manage to stick the landing before the tug pulled him too far away, it would be a matter of seconds or probably less, before the elastic tether would tighten up with the full force of the thruster-tug's substantial mass. He highly doubted he could maintain a single handed grip against such a force. It would rip him away from the hull and bounce him back to the tug. If that was ultimately inevitable, he might as well cut to the chase, by simply abandoning his current arcing trajectory right now, and pulling himself along the tether to get to the thruster-tug. In any case, it would be a lot easier to work if he had both hands free, but he could not lose the oboe. If only he had some duct tape! But the nearest roll of it was on the tug. At least there *had been* some on the tug. Who knew if it was still there? It could have been knocked loose by the impact or the explosion. He tried to look down to his waist, which is more difficult than one might think while wearing a pressure suit. He felt with his free hand instead. Yes, he had taken off his tool belt. It too, was on the tug the last time he had seen it. "Damn!"

Colin reached a decision. He tugged on the tether. At least this way he could control the amount of force, and therefore his speed, as he began approaching the tug. The speed of the launch equals the speed of the landing, after all. Best to keep what little control he had of this situation.

It's hard to be patient when you are floating gently away from your ship and toward what may or may not be a completely inoperable thruster-tug which itself is drifting slowly but surely into the depths of cold hard space. How much fuel remained in his suit's emergency thruster? If he couldn't get the tug started, he'd have to figure out how to get back to the ship. That was the whole point of why suits had emergency thrusters in the first place, but he wasn't precisely sure how long they were supposed to last, or how much he had already used. Of course, he could launch himself off the tug by jumping, but his own thrust might not even be enough to compensate for the outward drift of the tug, or more to the point, of the *him+tug* inertial reference system he was now already part of. The best option would be to jump first, providing as much initial momentum as possible, and then use the emergency thruster to supplement it. That *should* work. Good. It was decided then. He was still only halfway to the thruster-tug. Time was wasting, and distance increasing. The tether was slack, so he coiled it around his right forearm. It was an awkward move. He dared not try to use his left hand, lest he break or drop the oboe, so he could only use a weird stirring and spiraling motion with his forearm against the floating tether. It worked, basically, although it was a bit too tight in spots and too loose in others so that several loops slipped off and flapped clumsily. No matter. He tightened up the slack enough for another yank, adding a bit more momentum, and slowly tightening up the distance to the drifting tug. The new velocity seemed better. It should still allow for a manageable contact. He reversed his arm spins, shaking off the coils of tether. Then used a similar arm spinning motion to correct his orientation toward the tug. He wanted to land feet first so as to absorb the impact with his legs. He would then grab the roll-cage with his right hand, and settle himself into the tug's seat. Manipulating one's orientation using a single flailing arm is not as easy as it sounds. Overshooting is pretty much inevitable. Nevertheless, he made a valiant effort, and it was met with about as much success as one could reasonably hope for. He made the landing, absorbing most of the force with his right leg. It wasn't perfect or pretty. He stumbled a bit and smacked his right arm pretty hard against the roll-cage. It would leave a bruise, but no bones were broken.

A few seconds later he was in the pilot's seat, and he instinctively began reaching for the ignition button. Then he remembered his plan. First, find the duct tape. He breathed a sigh of relief as his eyes landed on a well-used roll jammed into one of the dashboard slots. "Thank all the gods!" he muttered. He grabbed the roll, and an old rag from another slot. He wrapped the rag around the oboe as a protective padding, then held it against the side of his shin, and used the roll of tape to wrap his leg and the oboe like an Egyptian mummy. He would be some kind of crazy undead flying god of musical resurrection. That thought make him laugh. Sometimes he wondered if he was actually slightly insane.

Now, his finger hovered over the ignition. It was in this moment that he noticed the charring of the tug. The explosion had blackened her paint, adding another layer to her already rich patina. The ignition button, like the other controls on the main panel was slightly deformed due to melting. "Please don't jam. Please don't jam" he chanted. It didn't jam. The button depressed under his finger as normal, but still his heart sank as it did so without any response from the engine. "Come On!" he pleaded, as he tried the button a second time. This time, the engine cranked, and sputtered in typical fashion. She was an ornery old beast, but it was not yet her time to die. Nor his.

He revved her up and kicked on her primary thruster, leaning on the stick to spin her around. Back toward home he raced, perhaps a little too quickly, and her engine coughed in protest.

Proceeding toward sector F, he rode again past the forward sections of the Ventas-341. It was a mess. Gaping holes, ruined strut work. A small part of him almost wanted to cry. Deck C28A now matched the chaos of the surrounding sectors, hanging limply like a broken limb, a burnt and empty husk, scraped free of all value, all beauty. All the good it once held was gone forever, save for the oboe taped to his leg, and the girl who would once again play it. The girl waiting for him back on board the ship.

Chapter 52

In the back of Hannah's mind there was a small sadness. The conscious majority of Hannah's mind, however, was overjoyed. She held the rag-wrapped package, and she knew in her heart what her eyes could not yet confirm. Colin had managed to retrieve her most prized possession. It was the only thing she really cared about.

He had been coy about presenting it to her, starting with the bad news first. Her studio was all but destroyed. There had been an explosion, he had tried his best to contain her belongings. They had all slipped through his fingers, but somehow…

"I was able to catch…" He was pulling something from behind his back, and she knew already. A spark lit in her eyes. Something that had been dead.

Rising to her feet, she almost hugged him, but he was holding the wrapped object out in front of himself. "OH MY GOD! COLIN! I CAN'T BELIEVE IT!"

Colin only smiled. What could he say?

She unwrapped the package gingerly, then examined it closely. It appeared to be undamaged. "Thank you so much!" she said this looking him straight in the eyes. Now she did hug him, though briefly, and somewhat reservedly, due to the fact that she still held the oboe carefully in one hand. "This is just… I mean, wow. I really never expected to see it again."

"Well, play a song?" Colin suggested.

"Oh! Yeah!"

She held the oboe toward her mouth, licked her lips, and stretched out her face muscles. Then frowned.

What to play? What song could possibly capture this moment? Did she even remember any songs?

"It's OK," said Colin, reading the indecision in her expression, "just play anything. It's not like me and him are gonna notice any different." He hoped it sounded encouraging. He didn't mean to convey that he didn't care about her music choice. On the contrary, he wanted to tell her that he trusted her ability - her choice of song, and her mastery of her instrument. He wanted to tell her that she could play a single wavering note and it would be good enough for him. He would be happy to hear it. He really just wanted her to be happy - to find the joy in her own music. He wanted to say all those things, but instead he could only manage to smile stupidly.

It was enough. Closing her eyes, she brought the instrument to her lips and with her breath filled it with life. Long, sad notes emanated from it and seemed to fill the room with a tangible presence. The ghostly, animal-like cry was eerily haunting and beautiful, summoning within Colin a waking dream, almost a hallucination. Colin imagined pastoral scenes inhabited by extinct wildlife. It felt so real, as if he had actually been moved to another place, another time. Ducks with colorful plumage squawked and fluttered upon a gently rippling pond. Fawns stood at the water's edge sating their thirst after a joyful run. Songbirds swooped after swarms of flying insects, and perched upon tree branches to digest their meals.

Presently, the tune ended, and the daydream faded, returning the listeners back into reality. Hannah remained quiet, with her eyes closed. Colin and Brother Anderson looked at each other briefly, each checking the other to verify their own strange feelings. Apparently, even the robot was experiencing the strange power of Hannah's music. A shiver flowed visible through his body.

'What just happened?' Colin silently mouthed the words to the robot, accompanying them with an exaggerated shrug.

The robot in turn, shrugged back.

Chapter 53

Hannah opened her eyes, and laughed, triggering a round of applause from her audience. Her soul felt alive, resurrected.

"Wow!" began Colin, "Hannah, that was incredible!"

Hannah grunted dismissively. She still had trouble accepting compliments.

"No really, I mean it." He glanced again at Brother Anderson, "Both of us, were… well… It was like some kind of enchantment or something. Hannah, I… I saw things."

"What? Like a vision?" Hannah dismissed the idea.

"Yeah - exactly!"

"Oh yeah. Whatever!"

Colin was unsure what else to say. He stared at the robot now for assistance.

Brother Anderson got the hint, but rather unhelpfully, he launched into a long, and overly clinical explanation of the philosophical state of current research findings in the fields of musical phenomenology and physiology.

Now it was Hannah and Colin who could only stare at each other.

"Really?" Colin jumped in, cutting the robot short, "I have no idea what you are talking about, man."

"Oh. I'm sorry. Yes, that was a bit much," the robot apologized. He had allowed his information driven mind to ignore the social cues. He was a bit distracted, and not quite feeling normal. Maybe he needed a reboot. The fact of the matter was that he had experienced something strange that he could not explain or even accurately describe. Like Colin had said, it had seemed to be some type of vision. Except it was not merely a physiological phenomenon. How could it be? He lacked the human physiology to support such artefacts. It didn't make any sense. To Brother Anderson's mind, it had seemed as though he had been transported into another body, in another time and place. In some ways, this was almost more feasible than Colin's presented concept of visions. At least for Brother Anderson's robotic brain, it was theoretically possible to transplant his software and transport his awareness into another hardware infrastructure. In some ways, he had already done the opposite process. His mind had been upgraded in place, on the existing hardware platform that Brother Anderson called his body. A theoretical possibility, however, did not equate to a physical feasibility. Brother Anderson was not aware of any existing technology or proven naturally occurring phenomena that could allow the spontaneous transportation of consciousness, and certainly not one that would present as apparently instantaneous teleportation or dimensional travel from one time-space location to another, and then back again. Not that either time travel or teleportation were impossible. They certainly were not. This was an accepted fact. Both were practically mainstream technology, under certain conditions, within certain limitations. The very wealthy could already access wormhole technology, and on the other side of that portal, the spindown had become the world's most coveted resource, the rich and powerful fighting to control the present by controlling access to the past.

Brother Anderson's distraction stemmed from these troubling thoughts, as well as other pressing matters. He needed to discuss the comms situation with the others. They needed to check in with Central Operations Fleet Command. He had put it off too long already. Technically, the ship was supposed to auto-respond immediately upon restoration. Once that was taken care of, they would have a good deal of planning to work through together. The upcoming course correction would be very risky. They needed operational plans, and contingency plans, and emergency escape plans.

He shook his head. Hannah and Colin were talking. He hadn't heard their conversation at all. That itself was another serious indication of his mental state. He launched an immediate reboot routine.

Chapter 54

Brother Anderson booted up. Colin and Hannah did not appear to notice. He ran a complete self-diagnostic. He would need a battery charge soon, but other than that, all subsystems were reporting normal status. He felt alright.

Hannah and Colin laughed about something. Hannah reached out and lightly slapped Colin's forearm. Brother Anderson recognized the action as an indicator of social ease. The two humans were beginning to develop a friendship. This provided a sense of relief for Brother Anderson. Humans needed social connection, in order to thrive physiologically. Additionally, it was essential for the crew of a ship to develop bonds of trust in order to work together safely and effectively. And this skeleton crew was in desperate need of some effective teamwork.

"...it's pretty ironic though, I guess," Hannah was speaking.

"How's that?" Colin asked.

"Well, just that if I hadn't been - if I'd have been a normal person and hadn't always locked myself away in my studio, I'd be dead now. Just like everyone else."

Colin considered this silently. He was about to speak, when she continued, spurred on by an upwelling of emotion.

"I really miss my mom... I wish I could talk to her just one more time. You know, I'm not sure I ever told her I love her."

Brother Anderson listened with fascination and excitement. He couldn't believe his microphones! Hannah had just opened her heart in a moment of rare vulnerability.

This was an unexpected leap. This was a critical moment. This was an unprecedented opportunity to nurture and build that invaluable trust. But not for him. This moment was entirely up to Colin. Only he could refine Hannah's vulnerability into a trustworthy human connection. Brother Anderson prayed, "Please god help Colin say something comforting."

Colin's own thoughts internalized Hannah's statement of regret. He too was haunted by loose ends. Things not done. Things not said. He had failed to save Tommy and Scranton. He didn't blame himself - not really - but still. Then he had missed their funeral. He had not had the chance to pay his respects. And they were gone, and it was too late. Them, and everyone else. He had never verbally acknowledged or thanked Chief Bryce for his mentorship. He had never stood up to Tommy regarding his constant idiotic behaviour. He had never gotten the nerve to apologize to Stef and Suzzanne. On top of that, he would be unable to save the Ventas 432. The sense of impending dread was almost unbearable. His ability to act responsibly as a crewman to the ship was hanging by the thinnest thread. The ship would soon be in ruins. In his mind, a part of him treated it as a done deal already. Unavoidable and inevitable. He was getting ahead of himself, he knew. There was still a chance, however slim. He just couldn't get his rational mind to grip that slim thread. His grasp was slipping.

He pulled himself back to the present moment, realizing that Hannah needed him to be with her now more than ever.

"I know." He was trying to agree with Hannah. "All our friends... gone."

If he had owned a set of lungs, Brother Anderson would have breathed a sigh of relief. He smiled in Colin's direction.

At the mention of friends, Hannah thought first of Cherise. They had shared so many good times, many laughs. She missed those younger days of innocence. Cherise was still alive somewhere far away. Was she still innocent? Hannah could imagine her no other way. And then there was Suzzanne. Suzzanne who had loved Hannah's music, like no one else on the ship had seemed to. Suzzanne who had loved to sing despite her inability to carry a tune. Suzzanne who had loved to dance all night. Suzzanne had loved life in a way Hannah had never understood. Now she floated frozen in a dark, silent emptiness. Dead. Disrespected. Abused. It was tragic.

"How could you do that to her?"

"What? Who?" She had been talking about her mother, right? But… Huh? This doesn't make any sense.

"Suzzanne! How could you do that to her?!" she was pushing him now. She wanted to hurt him. She wanted justice. She began sobbing, and clumsily punching at him

Oh! She's talking about Suzzanne! Right, because they were friends. I shouldn't have used that word. But she's right. I deserve a beating. I never apologized for that night. I wanted to. I didn't know how. I should have just talked to her. Like I should talk to Hannah now. *Come on man, say something!* What was the question again? Why didn't I apologize to Suzzanne?

"I was scared. I guess I was ashamed," he stammered.

"What! YOU were! How do think she felt? FUCK!"

Hannah stormed off. There was nothing to kick, and she just barely managed to refrain from punching the wall beside the hatch as she ran past.

Chapter 55

Colin sat on a tall stool at his workbench in engineering deck. He was pretending to fix a small compressor. He had begun in earnest, and had taken it apart, laying its parts in a reasonably orderly fashion, spread across the workbench. Suddenly he allowed his head to drop, thumping the workbench with a thud and landing painfully on a small screw which cut his forehead. It bled slowly, forming a tiny puddle around the screw. Part of him wanted to cry. Part of him was fine with simply bleeding. Maybe he should just turn to liquid and flow down the drain into the depths of the ship, to be recycled, his useful parts reclaimed and broken into elemental components. If there even were any useful parts of him.

He didn't understand women. He didn't understand Hannah. He hadn't understood Suzzanne. He never would. Not Suzzanne anyway. That was for sure. That was impossible now. Hannah seemed almost as impossible. He had replayed the conversation a million times. What had gone wrong? What was she talking about? What had he even been talking about? He wasn't sure of anything anymore. It made him feel completely useless - an utter failure. She was literally the only person within a million miles, but she might as well be a million miles away. She might as well be an alien for all their ability to connect - to communicate. How was it possible for them to be this ineffective? How could they be this stupid? Correction - how could *he* be this stupid? He didn't want to imply that he thought Hannah was stupid. On the contrary, he knew she was highly intelligent. She was smart, and talented, and pretty, and deep down, he was sure, she was even nice, in her own way. She cared about the people who mattered to her. She was able to make connections with others. Not like him. God - what an idiot! What did he do wrong? It was impossible to know. Their conversation had crashed and burned as surely as a ship with a hundred tiny hull breaches. The root cause was ultimately unknowable. If he could go back in time, he would record the conversation. He could listen to it and try to figure out what he had said that had caused the explosive impact.

He was no time traveler. He would never have the millions of credits required for that kind of spending. He was not one of those lucky few who could go back for a fresh start. Besides, it didn't work like that anyway. The spindown couldn't jump you back a few minutes or hours. It was limited to discrete windows of opportunity with periods in the range of years or more, dependent on complex orbital variables. Even if he did have access to that power, it wouldn't help. He had no clue why anyone even bothered. It's not like anything could ever change. Not really. People are people. The world is the world. Everyone just has the same basic needs that they have had for millions of years. The same basic limitations too. Had any man ever understood women? Was this some artifact of history that evolution had never surmounted? Had his Neanderthal ancestors been just as stupid as he was? Would future generations ever learn?

His mind drifted into a dream state. A caveman with bloody, matted hair rose from the ground, a screw protruding from his skull. The caveman boarded a gleaming silver spaceship, blasting into space, then splitting into two, a mitotic amoeba ship, becoming twin ships with twin caveman pilots. The ships drifted apart on diverging paths, then both exploded. One caveman was able to patch his ship back together with a roll of duct tape. He flew home, received a medal of honor, married a beautiful cavewoman wife, and lived in a castle by a lake. The other caveman was thrown from his ship. He clumsily dropped his roll of duct-tape, and was sent to prison for wanton destruction of property.

Chapter 56

Brother Anderson decided to go talk to Hannah. But he would have to wait a little while at least, perhaps a half hour, to give her time to cool down.

As he waited he checked in on his tanglebase account. There was something strange going on there. It somehow related to the odd vision he experienced when Hannah played her oboe. He had rebooted, and everything looked normal, yet somehow, something still felt a bit off.

Yes. This was strange. There was still a process running in the tanglebase. It was a copy of one of the low-level ship diagnostic routines. It included a bootstrap mechanism for offline use in extreme cases. How was it still running? It had been hours since he first detected it!

He inspected it more carefully, gently prodding at its log files and then its memory space, attempting to reproduce its logical structure in his own memory. He changed a couple of digits in its memory cache, and watched how it responded. It was fascinating. It appeared to be diagnosing its own memory-bound environment. It was almost as if it mistook the small local segment of tanglebase for a hardware subsystem. One which it did not recognize. One which it was attempting to analyze operationally, so that it could infer diagnostic semantics.

He made a second copy of the whole thing, intending it to be merely a data snapshot to use for later comparison. He planned on tweaking a lot more of its memory. To his surprise, the backup copy also began to initialize as if it were booting up a new process. Essentially, that was exactly what it was doing. He still did not understand how this was possible. He left the backup alone, but continued to flip digits more or less randomly on the first copy. The program reacted unexpectedly to various changes, but ignored others. He found it fascinating. It almost seemed to be alive, and he found it both entertaining and strangely, compellingly needy. It needed him to flip those digits for some reason. It somehow enjoyed the process, the interaction. He wanted to keep playing with it, but by this time, it would be best to check on Hannah.

Chapter 57

Hannah was resting in berth E-11. Brother Anderson knew she was resting because her heart rate, breathing, and body temperature had fallen to within normal resting range. The location part was not quite as precise. Typically, it would be, but most of the ship's subsystems were barely functioning, and personnel monitoring services was one such subsystem. In fact, all he could really tell was that she was somewhere in sector E. Had there been anyone else alive in the vicinity their signals would have obliterated one another but, things being what they were, at least this was one good thing.

Brother Anderson made his way toward deck E. He would not leave her alone like he had in the past. He only waited about an hour for her immediate anger to cool somewhat. Physiologically speaking, humans were for the most part quite incapable of overriding their own internal signaling mechanisms. A rush of adrenaline, ghrelin, or melatonin was a nearly unstoppable force. They were simple signals. Incontrovertible. Unmistakable. Not like words. So easily misunderstood. So prone to subconscious twisting. So reliant upon a myriad of multilayered infrastructural assumptions and expectations. So dependent on unspoken and unacknowledged social constructs. Constructs that he was only now beginning to grasp. Archetypes so deeply buried in the human psyche that no one had ever thought to explain them to a robot. A doctor. A priest. A servant. A brother. He would not leave her alone this time. This time he knew better. Presently, he knocked on the hatch marked E-11.

"Yeah?" Hannah asked.

"It's me," Brother Anderson replied. His robotic voice sounded different enough from Colin's that no actual name was required. Even through the hatchway the timbre and tone were easily recognizable.

"Come in, I guess."

The hatch swished open almost silently and his wheels rattled quietly over the threshold. "Are you alright?"

"Yeah."

"I brought you something." He held out a bottle of Roth's. He had debated this with himself. Perhaps it wasn't the best idea. She tended toward borderline addiction and overconsumption. However, as a social gesture, it could go a long way to build trust and help Hannah open up to him emotionally. She needed to talk to someone. She kept things bottled up inside until they burst. "I was hoping we could have a chat."

'A chat, eh?' thought Hannah. That's what assholes always call it when they are about to shit all over you. It's never a conversation, or a discussion. Always a chat. Like 'ooh we are so casual and cool, we're your buddy, your pal.' Give me a fucking break. Whatever. She was too tired to argue with this robot. Just let him say whatever it is he thinks he has to say. She reached for the bottle and took a long swig.

"Look, Hannah. I'm sorry. I focus too much on the task at hand. I'm very practical, as you know. It's how I am programmed. Honestly, It's what I am designed for. But, in my role, even as a robot, as a doctor, and as chaplain - well, frankly, it's not enough. I am trying Hannah. I am changing. I am trying to learn empathy, learn to feel things. My perceptions have been greatly expanded, you know. I think I can start to understand things that were never possible before.”

“Yeah?” She wasn’t convinced, but maybe there was something to this. He had changed a bit, she supposed. Was it possible for a robot to learn to feel? She doubted it. But it did actually seem like he was trying. Had he been a bit less of an asshole lately than he used to be? Still, why is he here? Hannah asked herself. Surely he did not bring her a drink just to sit and chew the fat. He wants something. He wants me to stop being mad. He wants to assuage my anger. He wants to control me. He can’t just let me be.

“I know why you are here, Brother. You think you can make me stop hating Colin, and play nice so we can all just get along.”

“I actually don’t know that I can do that, Hannah.”

“But you’d like to.”

“Of course I would like that. The fact is we are in trouble - all of us. We cannot afford to be divided when the ship is literally falling apart around us. Especially now. We have tasks we must perform and decisions we must make, and time is of the essence.”

“What are you talking about?”

“Hannah, you are aware of the communications shadow caused by the asteroid belt, correct?”

“Yes. Colin and I talked about that. We’ll be out of the shadow soon, right?”

“We are out already. I’m sorry, I didn’t mention it sooner. You and Colin were both asleep when we regained our connection, and then it was such an eventful day, I didn’t get a chance to say anything.”

“But you told Colin.” She meant the statement as an accusation, to expose the lie in his previous comment.

"No, not yet. I have not spoken to him since it happened."

Really? Hannah was pretty sure that couldn't be true. But it was not like Brother Anderson to lie so directly and explicitly. Was it possible for a robot to blatantly make a false statement? She didn't know whether to believe him. Could it be true that he actually would want to talk to her about it first. Did he trust her that much? Or care about her? Or whatever? It was weird. It was almost like Hannah was his friend that he wanted to talk to. It didn't make sense. "No shit?"

"No shit, Hannah. You are the first to know."

Huh. "So now what?"

"Well, we are *supposed to* report our position and condition to Central Operations Fleet Command Center." He paused briefly before continuing.

"But?" Hannah read between the lines of his statement.

"But, I am not sure that would be an advisable course of action, and I would like to discuss it further with yourself and Colin, and come to an agreement on how to proceed."

"Except that I don't want to talk to him."

"Exactly."

"And I'm not going to! And you can't make me. And besides that shithead's opinions don't really matter to me right now!"

"I realize that."

"So?"

"So, I'd like to hear from you exactly why you are so upset with him."

"Fuck you! I don't have to explain myself to you or anyone else. I'm mad at him cuz I am, OK?! Cuz he's a fucking pervert, and I don't want to have anything to do with him, and here I am stuck on a fucking piece of shit spaceship all alone with him, and this fucking sucks, OK?!" She took a long draught of the vodkatini.

"Right. You have every right to feel that way."

"Good!"

"Because he's a pervert, apparently."

"Yeah!"

"Except…"

"What?"

"What if he isn't?"

"Well, we both know he is! You were there afterwards when he did that to Suzzanne."

"Yes. I was. She came to see me. You were with her."

"Yes - she called me to come meet her and go with her to see you."

"And she told you…"

"That Colin molested her."

"Specifically, that Colin touched her breast, correct?"

"Um, no. That he groped her on the dancefloor."

"Are you sure?"

"Yes!"

"But that is not what she told me."

"What?! Yes - it totally is!"

"Not exactly. I have archived audio files of her conversation with me. I can play back her exact words."

"Great! Play it!"

"Alright."

A young woman's voice was clearly audible and easily recognizable as that of Suzzanne. A wave of sadness washed over Hannah as she heard it. She nearly burst into tears. She would have, had she not been concentrating on winning this argument. What was Brother Anderson getting at anyway?

Suzzanne's voice continued:

"I was dancing with a few girls from navs, right? A couple of engineering guys bought us a drink, and they were dancing near us, but not really with us. Then this one dude, you know that guy Colin, with the wavy hair? Well, he is suddenly right in my face, and he's putting his hand on my boob, and his buddy is right beside him laughing at me. So of course, I slap him and push them both away, but right after that I start to feel super dizzy like I know I'm about to pass out. Those assholes slipped me a roofie!"

"See!? He put his hand on her boob. She just said so! Besides, I was there when you recorded that. I already know this, so what?"

"So was Suzzanne passed out when you met her?"

"No."

"And she was able to walk all the way down to med bay to come talk to me."

"I mean - she was staggering a bit, I helped her, but, yes."

"I wasn't really sure what she wanted me to do, but she made an accusation about being drugged. So I had to check her blood toxins."

"You took a blood sample?"

"Yes."

"I don't remember that."

"Well, I did, and aside from significant blood alcohol levels, there was no evidence of any other drugs in her system."

"So she wasn't roofied?"

"Definitely not."

"But Colin did grab her. He must have. Suzzanne wouldn't just make that up."

"But could it have been an accident?"

"How do you accidentally grab someone's boob?!"

"Well, I did talk to Colin about this. He said that his friend Tommy pushed him, and that he dropped his beer, spilling it on Suzzanne and accidentally touching her breast. He also accidentally elbowed Stef in the face."

"Oh. Well did Stef come to see you?"

"No, she did not."

"Well, that Tommy is a fucking idiot, so that part makes sense. And Suzzanne did reek of beer. I remember that was weird because she always drank Roth's. But Suzzanne's not a liar."

"I'm not saying Suzzanne lied, but what I want to ask you is this. Is it possible that perhaps Colin isn't lying either? Is it possible that the incident was actually an accident, as Colin claims?"

Hannah thought about it for a moment. Some of the facts seemed to fit into both stories. Both scenarios were totally plausible. A girl gets roofied and groped on a dancefloor. A guy has stupid dickhead friends that push him into a girl. But why were no drugs found in Suzzanne's blood test? And why is Colin acting like he did it? He said he was scared, right? That's a stupid excuse, but it's not a denial. What did he mean anyway? How does being scared make you grope somebody? That really doesn't make any sense.

Chapter 58

Colin woke. His face was flat on the workbench. A small screw was stuck in his face. It hurt. As he lifted his head, his hair pulled painfully. It was stuck to the tabletop in a smudge of dried blood. The screw stayed stuck on his forehead for about three seconds, then dropped, bounced off the bench, and disappeared into the ethereal shadow world where only tiny screws go, especially ones with no easily obtainable replacements.

His forehead hurt. His hair hurt. His brain hurt. His neck was so stiff he felt like he could barely move. Slowly, he began stretching it out, groaning loudly. "Oh god". He felt like shit. His mouth tasted and felt like an old sock. His head pounded. Was he hungover? He didn't remember drinking last night. He looked around. There was no sign of it. No alcohol bottles. He shuffled across the room, dragging his feet. Finding a case of water bottles, he downed one greedily, then opened another.

He left engineering deck, turning toward sector F. He wandered aimlessly, allowing his feet to propel him along familiar paths, between storage rooms and access panels that all seemed so irrelevant. The ship sighed and groaned as it heaved along through its predestined course, as if it shared his aches and pains, as if it too suffered a phantom hangover. He finished the second bottle of water, then not realizing it was empty, tried to take another drink, getting only a drop. He tossed the bottle over his shoulder carelessly. It had helped a bit though, he had to admit. He did feel a bit better. "Too bad there's no such easy fix for you though, old girl." he told the ship.

He listened more intently now, as if she would speak back to him. In a way she did. Each shudder, each growl originated from a specific resonance pattern that was occurring at a specific spot of the ship's substructure. Although this was not Colin's area of expertise, one could use the frequencies of the sounds to track down the location of structural weaknesses. He had heard Bryce talk about it often, how back in the day he had used this trick to patch up an aging cruiser. There would be no patching this time though. Bryce's old cruiser had been a commuter vessel, stopping at port after port. They had quick access to spare steel. Not like out here. No extra parts here. We're on our own. We're each on our own. A crew of misfits. Puzzle pieces that just wouldn't go together.

He walked a bit further, coming to a stop in front of a hatch marked "EMERGENCY ESCAPE POD." A thought crossed his mind. Escape would be so easy. He could disappear into the dead of space, and with a little luck maybe land in some godforsaken frontier outpost on some dusty old rock. Take on a new identity with some under the table labour job. Never have to face the consequences: of abandoning ship and cargo, of somehow being the only survivor when all of his co-crew ended up dead, of his stupid inability to talk to a pretty girl, of his incurring Hannah's wrath.

But no. He couldn't. He couldn't leave Hannah. He couldn't give up hope that somehow there might be some small sliver of a chance that Hannah might forgive him, learn to like him, maybe even someday grow to love him. He prayed it were so.

"Dammit," he realized, "I think I'm in love with her."

Another thought entered his mind. Escape, yes, but together. Take Hannah with him to that godforsaken little frontier outpost, and disappear forever. With her.

Chapter 59

Brother Anderson watched Hannah as her expression changed into a mix of confusion and clarity. She opened her mouth as if to speak, then shut it again, frowning.

"Hasn't Colin always treated you with respect?"

She thought about their interactions. Now that the doctor mentioned it, Colin had treated her kindly, despite her sometimes open hostility. He had always been willing to do things for her. Sometimes crazy things, actually. He had managed to get her oboe. In the process, the airlock had apparently ruptured and exploded. That sounded dangerous, right? And she had been too selfish to bother asking about that. What exactly had happened? Was he hurt? She didn't even know. She hadn't asked.

He had helped her learn to use a spacesuit. And she wasn't even really sure why. Why would he bother? Why did he let her go with him to the airlock? When she had asked, she had had no idea what was involved. He could easily have told her it was a crazy idea.

He had gotten her food, and supplies. He had remembered her favorite drink. He had gone the extra mile to get her nice clothes that fit well. What was it he had said about the bunny t-shirt? "you look great". He wanted to say sexy, she knew that. She did look sexy. She knew it. He definitely noticed. But he had tried to be respectful. And always as they talked, he spoke to her as an equal. As a person. Never like a sex object. Even though he obviously was attracted to her. He never pursued a physical relationship. She would have handed his ass to him on a platter if he had. He probably knew that too. She had assumed that was why he was acting nice. But maybe it wasn't just an act. She had never caught him staring at her the way a lot of guys did. She was very good at catching them. Which meant either he was even better at hiding it, or perhaps, there was nothing to hide. She doubted he could be that good. She hated to admit it, but the robot might be right.

Chapter 60

"Which way now, Brother?" Hannah stood at another one of a seemingly infinite number of oddly acute angled corridor junctions of sector F. She had been in this area only once before; the day Colin had taught her how to use a spacesuit. He had been patient with her, as she clumsily struggled to move in the suit. She had reminded herself of a toddler just learning to walk and hesitating at each unsure wobbling step. Thinking of it now reminded her of another thought. She was just about to ask the robot, when he interrupted her thoughts.

"Right."

This confused Hannah. Had he just answered the question she was about to ask? How could that be? Could he read her mind? It would not be a complete shock - she knew he was monitoring her sleeping patterns and medical conditions - blood pressure and that type of thing she supposed. But, reading minds?

"What?" she stammered. "How? - I didn't even…"

"Go to the right." Brother Anderson clarified.

Hannah burst out laughing. "Oh my god, you freaked me out! For a second there I thought you were reading my mind. I was just going to ask you something like 'Am I right to assume that Colin shouldn't have let me use that space suit without proper training, and that technically, he could get in trouble for that?', and then you said 'right' like 'yes, you're right'!" She laughed again.

"Oh. Yes, that is quite humorous. And yes, you are right to assume that."

It confirmed a suspicion she had tried to delay thinking about. Colin had taken unnecessary risks for her. He had done stupid things, in fact; made bad decisions for her sake.

"Brother", she turned to face the robot, "When Colin went out there and got my oboe - I know he said that there had been some sort of explosion - was he… hurt? or like, in danger?"

"Colin did not sustain any injuries on his extravehicular excursion. However, based on his physiological data logged during the period, I would conclude that Colin had been in mortal danger on no less than three distinct events, before returning to the ship."

"You're saying he almost died?"

"Yes."

"Three times?

"At least."

Hannah had no response. It was unfathomable.

"Plus the time he blew up the wall to get you out of the mess hall."

Hannah looked at Brother Anderson quizzically.

"He didn't even wait for the flames to stop before leaping through to save you."

She hadn't thought of that one. So four times Colin had risked his life for her. Clearly, he was not such a bad guy after all. She found it hard now to reconcile the idea of the Colin she knew, with the one presented to her by Suzzanne's story. And she knew her own experience to be true. She trusted her own experience, and, surprisingly, she even trusted the facts laid out by Brother Anderson. The facts had made it clear. Colin is not a creep. He is actually a really nice guy. And he almost certainly has a crush on her.

She had come down to sector F looking for Colin, to grill him. To get to the bottom of it. To ask him what was going on. Now though, she started to feel that she already knew the answer. But still a few things didn't add up. Why had he acted so strange about the Suzzanne thing? What was it he said? He was scared. Scared of what? Maybe he had had a crush on Suzzanne. In which case Hannah felt a little less good about his current crush on her. Yes, there were still questions that needed answering. She spun around and took the right hand corridor, with Brother Anderson following.

After a few dozen meters and a few more twists and turns of sector F's jumble of passageways, Brother Anderson spoke.

"We appear to be getting close."

"Ok. thanks," Hannah replied, then called out loudly, "Colin! Are you here?"

"Hannah?" came the muffled reply. "I'm over here by the escape pods."

Thirty seconds later, and after two more prompts from Brother Anderson about which way to turn, Hannah faced Colin in a narrow corridor between what appeared to be a storage locker, and an escape pod hatch. The hatch was open, revealing the interior of the pod.

"Going somewhere?" Hannah asked with only slightly detectable sarcasm, which Colin failed to detect.

"What? No! I was just looking!"

"Relax, I was teasing!"

Colin released an audible sigh of relief, but he was on edge, wary of any possible reproach from Hannah. He shifted his weight nervously.

"But I do have some real questions for you."

"Yeah, OK", he tried to force himself to face the fact that part of him did want to have this discussion, to clear things up between them, although he didn't relish the thought of how it could turn out, or the process itself.

"We should sit down though." Hannah suggested, peering into the pod. "Maybe in there? Is it safe?"

"Oh! Yeah, it's safe enough. Might be the safest place around now that you mention it." The ship moaned and shimmied as if to agree with his assessment.

The pod was pretty typical, as far as emergency pods go. Not that Hannah knew any better. She had never seen an escape pod - not in real life anyway; maybe pictures, she couldn't say for sure. It wasn't large by any stretch of the imagination. It had a bank of four slightly cramped looking seats on each side, with prominent orange safety straps and large clips you could operate with gloves on. On the far end was a control panel of some sort. Beside the screen and oversized button panel were a series of bulky levers.

"After you!" Colin offered, with a sweep of his arm. "But watch your head!" The hatch was low. Good thing he had said that. It was just the perfect level to trick you into not seeing it, then smashing your head.

Hannah entered the pod and sat in the first seat on the right. Colin entered and sat across from her. Brother Anderson remained in the corridor. It was unclear whether he would have fit through the tight corner and small hatch if he had wanted to.

Chapter 61

Colin stared at Hannah, seated across from him in the escape pod. He had a strange sense of deja vu, although, neither of them had ever been here before. It probably had something to do with his daydream a few minutes ago - shooting off with Hannah to hideout in a backwater colony and starting a new life - a simple life. It could start right here, in this pod. But what was he thinking?! He could barely even talk to her. His palms were sweaty now, with anticipation. He assumed she was pissed. She had sounded fairly even-keeled out in the corridor, but he knew she could turn on a dime. He prepared to get his head ripped off.

"So, I've been talking to Brother Anderson," she began, glancing through the hatchway at the robot doctor, then back across the pod toward Colin, locking his eyes. "He tells me that you risked your life for me."

"Umm…" Colin didn't know how to respond. Had he? He hadn't really thought of it that way. But in a way that was sort of true. But even if it were, what would he say. What was Hannah expecting him to say? Was this some sort of accusation? He remained silent for a moment, and Hannah continued.

"He tells me that when you were outside, and you got my oboe back for me, something happened that put you in danger?"

"Yeah…" he agreed hesitantly, "you could say that."

"And also when you came to get me from mess hall?"

"What? Oh, well, not really."

Brother Anderson interjected, "Colin, you intentionally detonated an uncontrolled explosion of unknown magnitude, then proceeded to leap through a burning wall of flame into an unseen area."

"Well I guess if you put it that way…" Colin laughed. For a second Hannah smiled. Colin tried to avoid her gaze, but felt his own drawn inexorably toward it, and soon restored eye contact. Damn, she was beautiful. Her dark hair fell across her forehead and down, partially obscuring her blue-green eyes in a way that somehow seemed to hold all the mysteries of the universe. Colin was spacing out a bit, he realized. He felt lost in those eyes. Had seconds elapsed?

"Why?" Hannah's question broke him out of the spell.

"Why?"

"Yes, why? Why risk your life for me?"

"It's nothing. Anybody would. It's just what you do. When someone is in danger."

"Hmm, well… maybe. Sure if their life is in danger I guess maybe. If they are a good person."

"If who is a good person? The person in danger? Or the one putting themselves in danger?"

"Hmm, yes. Exactly."

"So are we good people then?"

"I'm beginning to think we might be." Hannah smiled, and this time, so did Colin. There was a moment's pause before Hannah continued. "So… what about Suzzanne? She was a good person too wasn't she?"

Colin nodded slowly, "Yeah, she was, I think."

"But did you treat her that way?"

"Well… I guess not. I didn't get a chance, before…"

"Didn't get a chance?"

"Yeah. To apologize."

"For what?"

"Come on. You know already."

"What was it you did to her? Did you slip her a roofie and try to grope her on the dancefloor?"

"What?! No! Wait - was that what it was made out to be? That's not…"

Colin clumsily explained to Hannah what happened that night on the dance floor with Tommy and Stef and Suzzanne. As he did so, misunderstanding turned into understanding, and, as she began to let go of the anger and bitterness she had held for him, a long-sustained tension left Hannah, as if she were slipping off a heavy backpack. Subconsciously, she rolled her shoulders to stretch into a newfound freedom. Colin wrapped up his story.

"I did feel really bad about the whole thing though. I wanted to talk to Suzzanne about it, but I didn't think she would want to talk to me. Still, I was trying to work up the nerve, and then days passed, and then, well, that was when all hell broke loose."

A light dawned in Hannah's memory; Colin's voice reverberating, '*I was too afraid, too ashamed.*'

"Oh shit! You were ashamed of being too afraid to talk to her, to apologize!"

"Yes," he admitted.

Hannah broke into a strange mixture of laughter and crying. She rolled out of her seat, stumbled across the pod, and sat beside Colin, half leaning on him with one arm across his shoulder in what might have been the most awkward hug in history. Her emotions were contagious, and Colin too found himself sobbing, although he had not yet figured out why, or what exactly he was feeling, or really what was going on.

Chapter 62

They sat in the pod a long time; talking, laughing, talking some more. Hannah and Brother Anderson informed Colin about their passage out of the communications shadow. Colin was surprised that Brother Anderson had told Hannah first, but he wasn't upset at all about it. On the contrary, he thought he caught a sly look from Brother Anderson, indicating that everything had all gone according to plan.

In a way it had, which was strange to think, given that the ship was in ruins, and they were surrounded by chaos and death. But honestly, Colin felt happy - maybe more so than he ever had - sitting here talking to Hannah.

"So? What will we tell them?" she asked, referring to the communication back to fleet command. The three all took turns looking at each other. Finally, Brother Anderson broke the silence.

"It may not be in our best interest to divulge very much information. Especially not until we can better assess the stability of the ship after the required course correction."

Colin watched Hannah as the robot spoke. He sensed an unspoken question. Or rather, he sensed that there was something about the implications of the robot's comment that escaped her.

"We need to make a course correction to curve around from the asteroid orbit, to an eccentric solar orbit," he began. Of course, she knew that. Every school child learned the basics of solar and planetary navigation, though the actual geometries involved were too specialized for general consumption, and were therefore reserved for in-depth analysis relevant to chosen profession. What she may not know was the correlation between the thrust required to make the navigational correction, and the structural integrity of the ship. "Once we initiate that maneuver, there is a high risk that… well, there's no easy way to say this… The ship might not survive the maneuver."

Now the slight confusion on Hannah's face was replaced by confusion and no small amount of alarm. Her jaw hung open, and her eyes darted between Colin and Brother Anderson, who decided that perhaps Colin's explanation was lacking a certain subtlety, and that perhaps the touch of a more qualified counselor was called for.

"If I may, it's not quite as dire as it sounds. We are very well prepared for emergency evacuation, and there is very little risk of actual harm to our persons. We will be OK, Hannah. The biggest risk is loss of cargo. Essentially though, the cargo is the primary focus of the mission, so the mission of the ship is in jeopardy. It is for that reason that caution is advised in exactly what details to communicate to Central Operations Fleet Command Center."

"Oh. So… You are saying we should lie to them, so they don't think we screwed up their mission and hold us responsible?"

"Well, that is somewhat of an oversimplification but it essentially does correspond to my concerns. Right now, fleet command knows nothing about the ship's status. They have received no reports since we entered the shadow nearly a year ago."

"So they don't know that the crew is dead."

"Correct. They also don't know that there were any survivors."

"But they will find the ship's remains eventually," Colin interjected, "and even if we're not here, they'll track the logs, and they'll know we survived. Then they'll come looking for us."

"Exactly," agreed the robot.

"Surely they can't punish us for surviving!?" Hannah refused to believe the implication.

"Not for surviving, no. But for failing to accomplish the mission, perhaps. There is precedent for such a response. It is not public record, but there have been similar occurrences in recent years. Surviving crewmen have been held personally responsible after loss of cargo, which resulted in forfeiture of wages due to mission failure."

Both Hannah and Colin responded in minor outrage, Hannah with "that's ludicrous!" and Colin with "I knew it!"

"The legal grounds for these scenarios are entirely controvertible, and the previous cases were appealed of course, but these appeals merely resulted in lengthy and very expensive battle through the judicial systems. It becomes a war of attrition - a very one-sided one though, since, comparatively speaking, the opponents are not on a level playing field in terms of the ability to fund such a war."

"Yeah, as if any private citizen has any hope of out-spending the Ventas-Calir corporation's lawyer budget!" Colin shook his head.

"I cannot in good conscious allow either of you to be put into that position. It would be completely unethical."

"So what then. If the cargo fails, will you tell them we died in the maneuver?"

"I was thinking it would be best to not mention your presence at all, at least until we complete the maneuver successfully."

"How is that possible?"

"The report could be written in such a way that it states that the crew has been killed, but focuses more on the physical and operational status."

Colin thought about that. It could work. He was no expert on the art of operational communications, but he had seen more than a few reports of the type. Mission status updates were always forwarded to all crew-members. Most didn't bother to read them, but Colin usually scanned them at least. He liked to know the basic gist of how operations were proceeding, so that he could assist Bryce with determining preventative maintenance schedules and system repair downtimes. Such planning was actually the chief's job, of course, not his. But Bryce valued Colin's input on such matters. Colin had sometimes wondered if the chief had been grooming Colin for a succession plan. It seemed a bit silly to think that; surely the fleet had more mid-level management track engineers, but here on the Ventas-341 there was a large experience gap. Most of the engineering crew were young, with limited experience, and even more limited aspirations. Aside from them, there was one mid-career guy who was the laziest son of a bitch Colin had ever met. At any rate, he had read enough system reports to be able to pick out the automated ones from the handwritten. The CSO handled the majority of such reports, and they tended to read a bit dry compared to the ones written by a human crew member. Automated probably wasn't the right word, as the CSO appeared to actually compose each report from scratch, they were all slightly different, not just a cut and paste job. But still, they tended to sound a bit "roboty" if that was a word. If a robotic CSO were left to compose the upcoming report, it would not be out of character for that report to miss certain human factors, and focus on cold, pragmatic facts. And in the case of a loss of crew, the report would obviously HAVE to be handled by the CSO.

"Brother, I think this idea of yours just might work."

Chapter 63

MessageHeader=MTC-LRC.4029571.396823
Timestamp=567.3467.23.783
OriginatingVessel=VENTAS_CALIR.CS45.VENTAS-341
SubmittedBy=CRS.05623928.ACTING_CSO
Progress=PAYLOADON.RET.CORNAV
Requirements=NAV_CONF
Status = AMBER/RED

Hanna and Colin watched the pod's main terminal as Brother Anderson composed the message data.

"That's the easy part done," he spoke out loud. "Now for the body, I'm thinking something along the lines of…"

More data appeared on the screen:

IssuesList:
_ID01
_DESC=CREW_LOST
_SEV=RED
_ACTION=N/A
_ID02
_DESC=NAV_CONF
_SEV=AMBER
_ACTION='navigational coordinates confirmation required'
_ID03
_DESC=HULL_DMG
_SEV=RED
_ACTION=N/A
_ID04

_DESC=PAYLOAD
_SEV=AMBER
_ACTION='bulk payload loss imminent RISK=RED'
_ID05
_DESC=FUEL/SUPPLIES
_SEV=GREEN
_ACTION=N/A

"How does that look?" He addressed them both, but they both knew he was really talking to Colin. Colin twisted his mouth, read the screen, glanced at Hannah, then back at the screen.

"Seems pretty good I guess."

"Any thoughts Hannah?" the robot asked.

"Uh, no not really. Except... that Action line, 'navigational coordinates confirmation required,' does that mean... are we lost?"

"Oh that? No. We aren't lost. That's just standard boilerplate stuff," Colin reassured her. "It's just that standard operations protocol insists on a coordinate check before and after any major course change. It's a safety thing, designed more for crowded shipping lanes, to avoid collisions and that kind of thing. Still, even way out here in no man's land, it is quite useful. A slight miscalculation can end up costing days or even weeks of travel time and fuel. It never hurts to get a second opinion."

"Except when time is of the essence," piped in Brother Anderson.

"Which it isn't," said Colin. What was the robot implying? Did he have that little trust in the ship's remaining integrity? And if so, why wouldn't he have discussed it with Colin instead of making an insinuation like that. It annoyed Colin more than a little, but also disturbed him. It was time for him to do another thorough inspection of his own. "How long will it take to get a reply anyway, would you figure?"

"Best case scenario around six hours, but it depends on a number of factors, only some of which I have current data for. It could be up to twelve hours, or even longer."

"So in six to twelve hours we should expect to get the reply, including the coordinates. Then what?" Hannah asked.

"Then we should initiate our emergency protocols and begin the course correction maneuver as soon as possible." answered Colin, shooting Brother Anderson a dirty look as he accented the last four words.

Brother Anderson ignored it, instead asking, "So are we all in agreement then? Regarding the message, that is. Shall I send it?"

Colin and Hannah exchanged a somewhat nervous look, but one which included a resigned nod.

"Send it," they both answered in unison.

Chapter 64

Brother Anderson excused himself, citing some lame excuse or another. Something in the med bay he had to check.

Hannah looked at Colin.

"I guess we are officially dead."

"Huh?" Colin took a moment to engage his brain. "Oh yeah, right. What was it? 'Crew lost, severity red, no action required.'"

"Yes, something like that," agreed Hannah.

"Well I guess no one will come looking for us then."

"So we won't have to worry about going to prison or whatever. But... Colin, what will happen to us? Will we be stuck on this ship forever? It's not much better than prison in some ways."

"What? No - of course not! Look at this pod! It will take us somewhere safe."

"Really? Where?"

"There are a few mining outposts around here. I was thinking about this earlier actually. Maybe we could hole up somewhere out here and make a comfy little hideaway to live out our days."

"Oh you've been thinking about this, have you?" She teased. Colin did have feelings toward her. She could see that now. And she didn't mind him knowing that just maybe, she might be OK with that fact. But she couldn't give up the chance to make him squirm just a little bit.

"Well, I..." Colin started to defend his intentions.

Hannah laughed at his awkwardness and pushed him over on the seat, then he too chuckled at himself.

"Are you going to sweep me off to some desert island or lock me up in some tower to keep me safe?" She was mock beating him now with balled fists hammering down upon his shoulder in slow motion.

"I would never put you in a tower! But an island might be nice!"

"It might, actually. If it has a nice beach."

"Of course it has to have a nice beach."

"And fancy shops!"

"Yeah." The cold truth hit Colin. Survival in the mining colonies was not a simple matter. They would miss the amenities. Life out here was hard and dirty. He'd have to work hard, for a lot less pay than he was used to. His face turned somber. Even worse, these places were not the safest for a young woman. They would tend to be full of creeps and cretins. Tommy would look like a saint next to this lot. Perhaps the tower option was a necessary evil. No. They would have to stay away from the concentrated populations. But that was pretty much impossible. It's not as though you could go carve out a place for yourself in the wilderness. This wasn't earth. There was no readily sustaining natural environment, with food and water and fuel and building materials lying around just waiting for humanity to come along.

What was he getting himself into? He was lying to Hannah, to make her feel safe, but she was not safe. She would not be safe. And there wasn't a damn thing he could do about it. They were on their own on the fringes of civilization. A civilization that was not entirely pleasant, and less so around the edges. She hadn't seen the dark underbelly of mankind - its sharp teeth and grasping claws. Its insatiable hunger. Its utter coldness. Part of him wanted to weep. For humanity. For Hannah.

"What's the matter?" Hannah had noticed his body tense up and freeze.

"I… It's nothing," he stated, his face stony. He had no idea how to tell her his thoughts. How could he? It would destroy her hope. Maybe they shouldn't even try this stupid plan. Where would it get them? At least here on the ship the only thing to fear was death. Anywhere else they could go, she would run the risk of far worse fates.

"Colin! Don't bullshit me! What are you thinking about?"

"I can't. This is a bad idea."

"What, the pod?"

"Yes. Well, no. Not the pod itself, but where it will take us. Hannah, there are no islands, no beaches. There is only darkness, and treachery, and meanness, and greed. There is only hard work, and hunger, and poverty, and theft, and exploitation. I'm afraid Hannah. I can't keep you safe out here."

"So we go somewhere better!"

"The pods are short range. It's not like we can fly off to Neptune or Uranus."

"I'll fly off to your anus!" She couldn't resist that tired old joke. It worked. Colin laughed quietly. It was one of the things she liked most about him, his sense of humour. It was dry and hidden most of the time, but like her, he respected the classics. The stupidity of a bad pun or the all-time dumb and slightly dirty humour. It was a strange bond between them. They were silent for a moment, enjoying the brief moment for a smirk.

"OK so the pods take us to wherever, then we hop the first transport to anywhere better."

"Right." His voice betrayed his complete unbelief in that possibility.

“What? Why not?”

“How?”

“What?”

“How?”

“They do have transport stations, don’t they?”

“Of course!”

“So what’s the problem?”

“What’s the problem? We’re dead! We’re cut off! All our accounts are closed. We no longer exist. Ghosts got no credit!”

“Oh… I see now. Yes. That would be a problem. But Colin! We’re not dead yet!”

“What are you talking about?”

“All we did was tell fleet that we are dead, right?”

“Yeah. And they’ll flag us, and that will lock down our official records, and our access, and our data. And our credit.”

“But they haven’t done it yet.”

“Wha…? Oh! They haven’t even received our message yet!”

“Exactly!”

“So we have at least a few hours to do something about it!”

“Yes! We can empty our accounts, back up our data, and then… well, I’m not sure.”

“Maybe we need to create some fake identities?”

“Yeah, maybe. Do you have any idea how to do that?”

“No. But I bet our doctor can find out!”

Chapter 65

"Brother Anderson!" Hannah and Colin both shouted, as they entered med bay. Colin allowed Hannah to continue,

"We have an idea, and we need your help!"

"Yes?"

"Well. We were wondering. Before we are officially recognized as deceased…"

"You would like me to backup your accounts."

"Yes."

"Already done. I have saved a copy of all your datasets to my own personal tanglebase account, or should I say, one of my replicated accounts."

"Oh really?! You have multiple accounts? Isn't that… sorta illegal?" Hannah did not know much about the technology or legal implications, but she was pretty sure about that at least.

"For private citizens yes, it is illegal. But corporate law differs substantially, with a lot more grey areas."

"So you're considered a corporation?"

"Not exactly. Technically I am considered corporate property. I am partly covered by corporate asset and excise law, and partly by software copyright. Neither of these are particularly similar to civil law, so my rights and expectations differ somewhat from those of a human. In a case such as this, these differences allow for a great degree of flexibility for someone such as myself."

"You're above the law! That's so cool!"

"It might be more accurate to say I'm beneath the law, but your point is taken, and is for the most part true."

"Wow! So that's awesome! And you already know how to create fake accounts…"

"They are not fake though. An account I create is just as real as any."

"Well, yeah, but you know what I mean."

"Do I?"

"Yeah, like without a person attached."

"Ah, yes. So here is the crux of the matter. You are correct to assume that a person must be attached to every account and that each person may only be attached to a single account. However, there is a surprising degree of flexibility inherent in the definition of personhood. In many ways, a corporation is equivalent to a person. And so is a robot, but only in some ways, as we already covered. I recently discovered that it is possible for a robotic personality to become multiple persons within the tanglebase itself, and these persons were what enabled me to create my multiplicity of accounts."

Colin jumped in, "Are you serious!? Are you saying you created a virtualized version of yourself?"

"Not exactly. That, as you know has been a long sought after goal of robot design, and I wish I could say I solved that problem, but no. Rather, by a form of happy accident and my own carelessness, I inadvertently copied a chunk of operating programming into my tanglebase account, which surprisingly, continued to run and was able to build a new memory space for itself. It was only possible due to my rather odd situation of having to run CSO firmware on top of my rather limited personal assistive hardware, something that no one would normally think to try, and frankly is highly inefficient. I must point out that the newly spawned persons are really only a tiny fragment of myself. They by no means resemble in any way what you might call my personality. They are a very thin shadow of my own programming, but they include just enough metastructure to supersede simple software programs. They are essentially operating systems designed for self-operation. The original version was simply a standard low-level bootstrap mechanism designed for ship diagnostics. I have been interacting with them over the past few days however. They are so much more than that now. They have become my house pets. I think of them as 'archaea'. They may or may not meet the criteria of living beings, but then again, the same might be said of myself. I would like to offer these archaea, with their related accounts, for your permanent use. With them, you may forge new identities."

Brother Anderson felt a strange sense of triumph mixed with loss. He now imagined the archaea as his children, and he was sending them out into the wide world to fend for themselves. By handing them over to Hannah and Colin, he would have to give up his own connection to them. He could try to hold onto it. It was completely feasible from a technical perspective, possibly even advisable. But for some reason, he knew he must relinquish them - hand them over in their entirety, and sever ties. Any less would be an impingement on Hannah and Colin's freedom, rights, and personhood. In this way though, it would be like a marriage. He was losing his archaea children, but in so doing he was gaining two human children. Hannah and Colin would somehow become his daughter-in-law and son-in-law. His hands shook almost imperceptibly as he reached out to take the hands of Hannah and Colin in his own.

Hannah looked at the face of Brother Anderson. It was not a human face, but behind it she sensed now a human soul. She recognized compassion and sacrifice. She recognized human dignity, the human spark of imagination, curiosity, creativity, and the quest for advancement. She recognized love. A single tear slid down her cheek as she squeezed his mechanical hand.

"I love you, Brother."

Chapter 66

Several moments became an eternity. The three spacefarers holding hands as they drifted amongst the stars. Then the moment passed, and mundane matters snapped them back to the needs of the day.

Colin cleared his throat. The others dropped hands and shuffled awkwardly.

"Um, sorry. That was nice. But yeah. So... you copied our data to your... archaea?"

"They are your archaea now. But, yes."

"OK. Cool. I mean, that's great! So, we'll need the logins I guess."

"Actually, I temporarily attached them to your existing account, so you can login as usual and check everything out, and then I'll detach your old accounts."

Colin moved to a nearby console and swiped in with his fingerprint. "Will the biometrics still work, once they kill us off?"

"They should. I programmed the archaea to copy your biometric data upon login. Although, let's verify your actual passphrases now just in case there are any issues."

Hannah walked toward another terminal.

"Oh, Hannah. I took the liberty of attaching your mother's account to yours as well."

"Really?! Isn't that kind of risky? She has... I mean had access to really high level stuff right? Couldn't that be, um... well, I mean, I'm not sure I want to see all that."

"That's perfectly understandable. I will delete her corporate records and leave only her personal files and financial accounts."

Colin spun on his heels. "Holy shit! You get your mom's bank accounts?!" Colin stared at Hannah in disbelief. Hannah in turn stared at Brother Anderson.

"Of course," he replied. "You are her legal heir."

"But she isn't even dead yet! I mean, technically."

"But we know she is," replied Colin, "and once we're dead you will cease to be heir, so the account would probably succeed to the company."

"No way! She would never let that happen. She's have some kind of backup charity or something for if it couldn't go to me for some reason."

"But Hannah. It *can* go to you. It *has* come to you already."

Hannah thought about that. It felt weird, and wrong for some reason. Why did it feel so weird? She felt like she was stealing. Her mother had been diligent to instill into Hannah a strong sense of certain ethics. You worked hard. You didn't lie unless you had to. And you didn't steal. But maybe Colin was right. Of course her mother would have willed everything to Hannah, of that she had not a doubt. She could even check her personal files, now that she had them, but she knew it would be a waste of time. Absolutely, one hundred percent, Hannah was Maison Bhutros's sole heir. So it wasn't stealing. The account was legitimately hers. Turning slowly, she finished logging in, and opened her banking tab.

"So, coma boy. About that beach…"

Colin jogged across the room to look at her display.

"Ho… Lee… Shit…"

Chapter 67

"So. We good to go?"

Brother Anderson had just finished tying up all the loose ends with their accounts and ensuring that the archaea had the correct access. He considered setting up a modest income stream from Ventas-Calir corporation, tied indirectly to each archaeon through multiple levels of corporate obfuscation. There were a number of relatively low-risk structures that could work, but in the end, he decided against it.

The problem was the risk, however low, of a paper trail that could potentially lead to Hannah and Colin. He was almost sure he had thought of everything, and could plan around any known risk. But there was still some inherent risk the idea. He did not know everything. Of course. No one did. No one could. There could be some weakness he was blind to. Some hole in his security strategy that might be discovered. No, there could be no trace. No breadcrumbs. Nothing that could blow their cover. He could not tolerate even the slightest risk if it could compromise Hannah and Colin's safety. As of this moment, he could safely guarantee the integrity of their new accounts. The archaea now formed the foundation of their accounts, and had no connection whatsoever back to the original accounts, which were now essentially empty shells, left behind only to give Ventas-Calir something to close down.

As much as it would have been beneficial to maintain a consistent stream of income, it really wasn't necessary. Hannah's mother had amassed enormous wealth by shrewdly investing the bulk of her handsome salary. Hannah was set for life. And so long as Colin stuck with her, he would be as well. He hoped they would stick together. Watching the two of them interact brought Brother Anderson a sense of joy. It seemed as though these two people somehow created a third entity that enveloped but somehow transcended their separate identities.

"All clear. Please test your biometrics one more time."

They both finger-swiped in successfully.

"Excellent. Now I need to run some ship diagnostics in order to prepare for navigational thrust. Colin, I will need your help shortly, as there are some manual steps involving engineering controls."

"Yeah, sure - Oh… But… Wait a sec. If the thrust process requires manual steps. Won't fleet control figure out that there must have been someone else on board besides you?"

"Yes, actually - and good deduction by the way - they would be able to tell from the ship logs; except that I am planning to purge the ship logs. The existing data already shows abundant evidence of your presence."

"Oh right, of course it does. So are we just going to destroy the whole log?"

"I would prefer to retain the original logs as much as possible. In particular, I feel it would be irresponsible not to keep a record of the hull breaches, with as much relevant data as possible. In fact, the quarantine and coincident medical records are also important to keep intact, at least up until a certain point. I thought of truncating the data at a certain point in time during that initial period."

"I agree. If fleet is ever able to retrieve anything from the wreck, they need to know what caused this. What it can do."

"Yes, precisely. I do however have an additional concern with this solution." He stopped short, somewhat strangely.

"Do tell."

Hannah glanced up at this. The tone of Colin's comment belied a secrecy that piqued her interest.

"Well. The relevant time period also will reveal the fact that CSO duties were passed to myself."

"What's wrong with that?"

"Well. My own personal concerns are much the same as yours regarding the wisdom of going into hiding."

Hannah jumped up "Aha! You've got a secret plan!" Her voice contained both joyful glee and cheerful mocking. "Are you also planning to find a nice beach to lie on and sip margaritas? Or could it be something more mysterious?"

"Ah, well, if those are my only two options, I'll have to go with 'something more mysterious!'" He actually managed to mimic Hannah's tone fairly accurately, with a somewhat creepy effect, causing them all to burst out laughing. Brother Anderson's laughter simulation was even more creepy than the original joke, and immediately became a new target for laughter.

Their frivolity was interrupted by a loud, extended groaning and grinding sound, followed by a shuddering tremor. At once, all three shut their mouths with a snap and instinctively cocked their heads in an attempt to locate the noise's source, but it seemed to come from everywhere. It was a truly horrible sound, more sinister than any imagined construct. It was a monster both very real and very close, in whose belly they were already encaptured, and whom threatened to vomit them out from that relative safety into the eager fires of sudden death.

They all glanced at one another, holding their breath and listening for any sign. Colin spoke first, in a whisper.

"Brother, can you get any detail on that?"

"The exact cause and location is unknown. Overall hull status remains relatively normal. No new hull breaches detected."

Again the monstrous groan shook the ship. This time, rather than dying off, the sound resolved itself into a slow repeating thrumming rhythm.

"Ah. It is becoming more clear now. A large section of sector B appears to have shifted. We would need visual inspection to confirm, but I suspect that the hull has peeled back, much like a banana. The continuing resonance indicates that it may be flapping like a flag in a breeze."

"Shit," Colin muttered under his breath. He hadn't meant to voice it aloud, not wishing to alarm Hannah.

"It's bad, isn't it?" Hannah had tried to ignore the technical points of their situation. Deep down, though, she knew. The ship was barely holding together.

Colin could not keep the truth from her. He nodded once slowly, looking into her eyes. They held a certain amount of fear, yet that fear was held at bay by a trust that welled up to fill iris and pupil. A trust he could not betray.

"Come on." The supply cart still stood where he had placed it nearby, less a few water bottles and protein bars. He began to maneuver it hurriedly toward the corridor. "We've got to get you to the escape pod! Just in case."

"But…" Hannah began.

"I'll join you in a minute, but we have to run some tests. I have to help Brother." He was pushing the cart down the shuddering corridor now. The cart, as if in sympathy with the ship, developed a shimmy in its front wheel, making it difficult to steer. Colin tried to kick the wheel back into place, while simultaneously herding Hannah subconsciously with one hand on her back, and trying to talk her through the plan. It was far too many items to multitask at once. The wheel became jammed, the cart shying off toward the corridor wall. Colin switched sides, moving to the front and now dragging the unwilling cart behind him. Hannah tried to help, grabbing the other front corner, and the two dragged the ornery beast along, pausing briefly as a box fell off the top, spewing its contents across the corridor behind them.

"Leave it! We have enough!" Colin ordered as Hannah began to stoop to the spilled goods.

The mess was a small challenge for Brother Anderson, who was lagging behind them slightly. He had to switch from rolling to walking mode to avoid the obstacle.

"Colin," he began, but was quickly cut off by Colin's agitated response.

"What!?"

"We might consider skipping the tests. I fear they may be a moot point now."

"I think so, too, Brother. Quickly now Hannah, this way." By now they had come to the twisting corridors of sector F, and Colin's guiding hand became less of an unnecessary instinct, and more of a useful navigational aid.

Hannah was barely thinking, just running. The jarring pace and the disorienting sonic wobble occupied her attention in a jumbled blend of pounding feet and blurred streaks of lockers and acute angles which seemed to jump out at her. She reached out for Colin's hand, and upon landing within it, she found a single point of firm stability upon which the spinning world could anchor. They ran faster now, yet the journey was smoothened. Each upcoming corner was tamed from an unknown obstacle, to a simple course correction. She could anticipate now, which direction they must turn. She felt the location of the pod ahead drawing them to it.

Chapter 68

Colin was helping Hannah settle into the escape pod. They had scant few supplies. There was ample food and water, but that was the extent of it, aside from the first aid and emergency gear already on the pod. He debated going to E-11 to fetch Hannah some extra clothes. He didn't want to leave Hannah though. The decision was made for him when a notification alert dinged softly and Brother Anderson spoke.

"We have just received the response from Central Operations Fleet Command Center. It contains the navigational coordinate verification codes. I am sending them into the navigational subroutines now."

"I guess this is it huh?" Hannah reached for Colin's hand.

"Before we proceed, there is one other matter…"

"What is it Brother?"

"I don't quite know how to say this… Hannah. The archaeon… have you… can you *feel* it?"

"Can I feel it? Like, in, er, on my account?"

"Yes."

"Well, I… I mean, I haven't really had time. I literally was logged in for like a second."

"Oh. Of course. Well. I wonder. Could you do something for me. Later, I mean. I'm sending you an executable program, it should be in your account now, titled '*archaeon3*'."

"OK…"

"It contains my account details, and it will essentially repeat the process I used to create Colin's archaeon from yours. Yours was the first; the spontaneous one. Colin and I will be your progeny so to speak."

"Um, that's kinda weird."

"Hannah, I feel as though this archaeon might somehow keep me alive in away."

"What are you talking about!? Aren't you coming with us?"

"No. I can't. Even if I could fit inside the pod, it wouldn't work. I need to be on ship in order to carry out the next procedures."

"Brother, you're wrong!" Colin jumped in, "You can partially disassemble, and trigger and control the navigation maneuver from the pod."

"You're right, Colin, but once the maneuver is complete, I need to send the confirmation transmission."

"Yeah. Which you can also do from the pod."

"True again, but only if the pod is still docked."

"Right, so… oh." In all probability, the maneuver would tear the ship apart. This was as close as Brother Anderson had come to admitting it.

"It's best this way, Colin. I will go down with the ship. I must do that - but thanks to Hannah, I may be reborn."

"What? I don't really…" Hannah looked at Colin. Did he know what the robot was talking about?

"Hannah, I am a robot. I'm a bucket of bits. My life is no great loss. No more than turning out the lights at night. But you have made me something more. Your fury, your stubbornness, your music. You have taught me to love. I do not truly know what has happened to me, but I know that you are a part of it, and you too, Colin. Something has awakened in me that frankly should not exist. Cannot. I don't know. But I'm trusting you. If you did it once, you can do it again. Let me die and be reborn. Please."

Hannah stepped out of the pod, ducking around boxes of supplies, and the low hatchway. Tears dripped off her cheeks as she reached out to hug the robot. She squeezed him like she had not squeezed anyone in years, her mother had been the last, and probably the only one.

"OK, Brother. I will do this for you."

Chapter 69

Colin sealed the hatch of the escape pod and locked the interior manual latch. Hannah peered over his shoulder toward the robot, barely visible through the small plasglass pane. She still did not really understand what she had promised him. Of course, she would do it. She was glad to be able to help in whatever way she could, but the actual effect of her actions was somewhat fuzzy. Somehow, the program she had would allow Brother Anderson to reboot or rewrite himself into the tanglebase. That sounded a little sketchy to her, but he seemed convinced it could work.

Through the plasglass, Brother Anderson gave a curt salute, then disappeared. His voice came through the control panel on the pod.

"I am heading to engineering bay now, to initiate the navigational maneuver."

"OK," Hannah replied. She was sitting next to the console so she could reach to press the transmit button. She released the button, then spoke to Colin, who was now moving to seat himself across from her. He picked up her pressure suit and passed it to her, then picked up his own.

"Do you need a hand with it?"

"I should be OK, at least… I might need help with the helmet, I guess."

"Sure thing." He had one leg in already, and slightly lost his balance, as he tugged on the suit. He managed to avoid toppling over onto the seats, but Hannah took the opportunity to rib him.

"Are you sure YOU don't need a hand?"

"Ha ha."

"I'm approximately halfway there," came the robotic voice over the intercom. They both had their hands full with their pressure suits, so neither could conveniently reply.

"This is so crazy!" Hannah told Colin.

"Putting on a spacesuit is crazy?"

"No. I mean the thing with Brother Anderson."

"I know."

"Can he really… I mean, is what he is talking about even possible?"

"The thing with the archaea you mean?"

"Of course that's what I mean."

"Is it possible? Well. Honestly. I don't know. In some ways, sure why not? After all, a robot is just a program really - well, a big collection of programs, and in his case a rather complex one. We tend to think of the robot's body as an integral part of it, but is it really? It provides a hardware framework to run on of course, and lots of sensory interfaces, but none of those are really intrinsic to the programming, and for the most part, certainly not mandatory. But I don't know. Simple robots can be cloned and copied and moved across hardware no problem. But Brother Anderson seems to be more than just some simple false persona. I almost wonder… He seems to have changed from before - when he was just the doctor, he was the same as any old medical robot. But now…"

"I know, right?! He's not the same, Colin, I know he's not! And he's not just a robot anymore!"

"Yeah. Somehow, I think you're right."

"And he knows it too!"

"Yeah."

"So if that's true - is he alive? Like really?"

"Hmm. Maybe."

"So what if his idea *doesn't* work?"

"Well…"

"Colin, I'm worried - I don't want him to die!"

"Yeah, of course! Me neither. But… Well, he seems to know what he's doing."

"I know, but…"

"Well, if he really is alive, then… well… we need to let him make his own decisions. And besides, he is right about staying on board. It is his duty. He's high ranking officer."

"But only if he's human!"

"Huh? What do you mean?"

Hannah paused, not just for effect. The idea was bubbling up from her subconscious, and just now taking form. She hadn't really thought about it much, but now the effect was becoming clear, and in so doing, it clarified the cause as well.

"Colin, *you're* high ranking officer!"

"What?! No."

"Yes, you are."

"What are you talking about?"

"What's your current rank?"

"Chief of Engineering. It's not that high a level. And I only had to take it so someone could make official decisions on technical details."

"Really? Like what. What official decisions?"

"I don't know! Like… status reports and stuff."

"Which you have done?"

"Yes! I've run a bunch of reports. You've seen some of them on screen, remember all the yellow ship sections?"

"Sure."

"So?"

"So, has Brother Anderson been asking you to sign off on all his reports?"

"No."

"And what's his rank exactly?"

Colin thought about it. "Well, he's CSO, but that's not really a rank, is it? It's a system designation. He's Chief Medical Officer, I guess. Well, plus Chaplain, so that's two pretty much equal ranks, same level as mine."

"But you're a *human*! Doesn't that outweigh any robot?"

"Um. I guess it would. I don't really know."

"Colin, he tricked you! He's known all along! He knew he was human, and he knew he could let you think he outranked you, and that one of you would have to stay with the ship and that it would have to be him because he needed to save your life!"

"What? He's not human though."

"Obviously! But he's acting as though he is! And he's doing it to save you!"

"Get outta here." It was an obligatory argument, lacking conviction. "There's no way…"

He sat down hard. One arm still hung out of the pressure suit. His jaw sagged and he raised a hand to lightly touch his forehead. Could it be true? Maybe. Yes. Yes, it had to be. He was supposed to be Captain. He was supposed to be the one going down with the ship. He'd been fooled. Fooled into a lifesaving circumstance.

"You clever bastard!"

Chapter 70

"I'm in engineering bay now. About to initiate sequence. Are you folks strapped in?"

They weren't. They didn't even have their suits on yet. Hannah jumped to the transmit button.

"Hold on! We're not quite ready!"

Colin was waving frantically at Hannah as she released the button. "Don't tell him we know!"

"I won't! As if I would!"

"OK, I know, but, just…"

"God!"

"Sorry. I'm just trying to think this through. Hannah, if he knows I know I outrank him, he might feel that he has to bow to my seniority."

"He might."

"But in so doing, he would recognize me as Captain."

"Right."

"Which would mean…"

"He's in your position. A position you can't be in. I will not let you leave me."

"I don't *want* to!"

"Good! So we're settled then!?"

"Yeah."

"OK. Now let's suit up and get the hell out of here!"

"Well…"

"What now?"

"Let's suit up and *probably* get the hell out of here!" Colin grinned wryly. There was still a slim chance that the ship would actually survive the maneuver. If it did, they wouldn't have to escape.

"Hold on. I just thought of something." Colin cocked his head slightly. "We've been talking about probablys this whole time, but there's no probablys! We sent the message, remember? - Crew Lost! We're dead! There's no coming back from that!"

"Not for us." Hannah agreed. "Maybe for Brother. I hope so for Brother."

"Yeah, but at this point it doesn't matter if the ship survives or not! I've already abandoned my post!"

"Hmm. Yeah. I guess that's true."

"Fuck! I would never have chosen this, you know? I'm no deserter."

"I know. That's why Brother had to trick you."

"Shiiit." He shook his head in disbelief. "Wait! You put him up to it, didn't you?!"

"Colin no! I swear I had no idea!"

"I guess he tricked us both then."

"I guess he did." Hannah hopped up and down, tugging on the shoulders of her suit, adjusting it so it could close. They helped each other with the helmets, then buckled themselves in to the seats.

Hannah reached for the transmit button. It was almost out of reach. She adjusted her position slightly, then pressed the button.

"Brother. We are ready."

"Alright. Initiating nav sequence in ten seconds."

"And Brother, we are launching the pod now."

"We are?!" Colin stared at her incredulously.

"You are?" Brother Anderson replied.

"Yes, we are."

"Very well. Goodbye Hannah. Goodbye Colin."

"We have to, Colin," she told him, after releasing the transmitter.

He knew it too. The risk of damage to the ship was severe. Remaining attached only served to put them at risk. There was already no way to undo what they were about to do. They were committed to this escape no matter what. It was the only way forward.

"Goodbye, Brother." Colin said.

"Oops." Hannah burst out laughing. "I need to push the button, silly!" They both laughed, then regained their composure. "Ready?"

"Yeah."

Hannah pushed the transmit button a final time, then signaled Colin. They both said it together.

"Goodbye, Brother."

Releasing the button, Hannah looked to Colin. "We'll see him again, right?"

"Yes. We'll see him again."

"Now, for your button, Colin."

The pod launch release control was actually a lever, not a button, but Hannah didn't know that. He first flipped a few switches to enable all pod subsystems, and switch over from central ship command. A couple quick glances at status indicators showed all was working correctly. He moved his gloved hand to the lever, hovering over it briefly. "Ready?"

"Yes."

Pulling the lever, he released the pod. He released himself from former obligations. He released them both from ship-bound living, from life as they had known it up until now.

Chapter 71

The final seconds counted down. Then from deep within the ship's structure, a rattle erupted, followed by a deep roar that overpowered all the other sounds. The whole ship shook violently. In engineering bay, loose objects rattled off the workbenches, cascading to the floor in a silent cacophony. No sounds could compete with the mighty roar of the ships engines. They had idled at five percent output for so long, Brother Anderson had almost forgotten the experience of their full power. It was an amazing phenomenon.

The new coordinates popped up on his perception, requesting final approval. He confirmed. The ship began to swivel her enormous mass. Fifty million tons of ore resisted the force. Fifty million tons of ore wanted to maintain their current trajectory. The roar of the engines sought to convince them otherwise. The hull shook and bucked like a wild beast, and though its hideous groans could not be heard beneath the engine noise, Brother Anderson could feel them, could see them on his data visualizations. The entire hull appeared red in his view. Then suddenly, the hull was no longer a single structure, but a chaotic mass of giant steel ribbons, thrashing to and fro', in an explosion of red, blue, and green data. The instantaneous release of tension tricked the system into displaying many of the structural components as within normal tolerances. The tolerances may have been normal, but the shapes certainly were not. The Ventas-341 had been torn into a tangled matrix of no particular shape. A chain reaction of explosions was now spreading through her interior spaces. She had become a giant fireball. Brother Anderson sensed the heat behind the engineering bay hatch, even before the wall in front of him ripped in two. Negative pressure sucked his steel and plasmold body through the gash, hurling him past horribly twisted struts amidst flying panels and various debris. He was singed slightly as a fireball shot across his path. Suddenly, he was surrounded by millions of tons of rock, as the momentum of the cargo carried it past him. It was spreading out along its original trajectory, the containment fields now gone. The cargo became a huge three dimensional field of gravel. As he fell through it, he felt as though he was tunneling rapidly through a planet, as the planet was falling apart. Then the debris field spread behind him as he rocketed from its space. Behind, and to his left, the giant engines still spewed their blue plasma out in a mighty jet, but that jet was now losing shape as the various engine components fell apart from each other, their individual plumes now crossing and interfering with one another, driving the still burning engines through the debris field and beginning to melt the cargo to slag.

Even as the ship and payload continued to disintegrate all around him. Brother Anderson had one last task to perform as CSO of the floundering Ventas-341.

All monitoring systems had now failed to function, so there was no way of knowing if it worked, but he had to try. He composed a final message to Central Operations Fleet Command Center.

MessageHeader=MTC-LRC.4036728.937465
Timestamp=567.3694.04.289
OriginatingVessel=VENTAS_CALIR.CS45.VENTAS-341
SubmittedBy=CRS.05623928.ACTING_CSO

Progress=PAYLOADON.RET
Requirements=N/A
Status = RED
IssuesList:
_ID01
_DESC=VESSEL
_SEV=RED
_ACTION=N/A
_ID02
_DESC=PAYLOAD
_SEV=RED
_ACTION='payload loss remediation req'

He launched the send routine. That was all he could do. It would not even be able to tell him if it transmitted successfully. The inter-component communications were not responding. Most likely the control unit was destroyed. Most likely the transmitter was destroyed too. Everything was destroyed. As he would soon be.

It was over.

He launched the data deletion routine. It prompted for authorization. He spoke his passphrase - but stopped short before the last syllable. It would wipe his memory, delete all his local data, terminate his original incarnation. Disconnect, delete, destroy. He would be no more.

For a while.

Until Hannah's promised resurrection.

Hannah will spawn my third archaeon.

He took one final look around. The vast expanse of space stretched before him. Robots were not supposed to wax poetic, not supposed to feel. Sadness, immensity, awe, ecstasy, love, hope.

At the edge of his field of vision he noticed a speck among many, a speck with a telltale shape. The shape of a Kernighan TS17 thrustertug. It was far away, but not too far. Its trajectory was vaguely parallel to his own. He had an idea.

His local data storage still held a copy of the ship's log files. He traced back to the moment of the initial hull breaches. Yes, here it was.

EventHeader=SEC-NAV.376.13428
Timestamp=567.3297.17.824
_User=SFELD446
_Type=security protocol
_Description='emergency navigational beacon launched, channel 569.2043'

He set his telemetry to scan the channel indicated in the log. Yes. There it was. The beacon was still active. Unbelievably, it hadn't met the fate it warned of. It had not yet bumped into any of the deadly motes.

A small chunk of rock bumped his elbow. With his other hand he scooped it up, plus a few more that floated through his vicinity. He collected them in his left hand, and then, taking one into his right hand, held the pebble between finger and thumb. He estimated its mass. Then, with as much momentum as he could impart to it, he flicked the pebble away, in the direction opposite from the thrustertug. It flew away fairly quickly. Yes. This could work. It would take many, many flicks of many, many pebbles. It would take quite a while to close the distance, but there were plenty of pebbles floating nearby which he could continue collecting along the way, and he had nowhere else to be. Nothing better to do. He laughed out loud at the ridiculousness of his situation.

Eventually, Brother Anderson did reach the thrustertug. He programmed it to automatically navigate toward the emergency beacon, then set thrusters to full. It would be another long journey, but this time it would not be one he would remember. He would not be aware of his own presence when he reached his destination. He would not see the green and yellow fluorine reactions. He would not notice as his chassis exploded through the cloud of deadly debris. He had miraculously sailed unscathed through fireballs and shrapnel and tons of grinding rock. This next collision would not be one he would survive.

He returned to the data deletion routine. The original confirmation thread had timed out, so he launched it again re-using the parameters he had already fed it. Then he spoke his passphrase, one last time.

Chapter 72

The pod blasted away from the Ventas-341 on her small thrusters. The plasglass pane showed a wall of dark grey, receding rapidly, then a glare of light as sunshine hit the pod, now out of its mother's shadow. The warm sunlight lasted about two seconds, giving Hannah and Colin just enough time to really notice it, before being replaced by an orange ball of fire much closer than the sun could ever be.

The pod was buffeted as a minor shockwave raced past her, followed by shrapnel and fragments of former hull. A few bangs and crashes caused their hearts to race as bits of ship ricocheted off the pod's thick hull. It was tough, though, built to withstand atmospheric entries and even crash landings. They were safe here. A few more seconds later, the new found silence allowed the passengers a chance to relax into their seats and their breathing.

"It's OK. We made it. The worst is over with."

"Mm-hmm." Hannah nodded, her breath was forced as she willed herself to relax. Finally letting go of her safety straps, she reached for Colin's hand.

He saw the nervousness in her eyes, even through the slightly fogged up helmet. "It's OK," he repeated slowly.

"I know." She was starting to believe it now.

Colin just held her hand for a moment, then he tapped on his own helmet. "I guess we can take these off now."

"Are you sure?"

"Yeah." He cracked the seal and pulled off is helmet, then helped Hannah with hers.

"Wow." Hannah shook her hair loose.

"Yeah."

"So, uh. Where are we going anyway?"

"I guess we never really got a chance to sort out which of those beaches we are hitting first, eh?"

Hannah laughed, "Yeah right."

"Well, we are headed back into the belt, with the sun at our back, and there's plenty of places to go, not too far from here."

He was right. The sunshine was again beaming through the pane behind them. It made Hannah feel as though the pod was riding on a beam of light that would carry them to their destination, wherever that may be.

"Pass me my oboe will you?" She was wriggling out of her thick-gloved suit now.

"I don't have it. I thought you packed it."

"Shut up!" She slapped him with a flapping, empty glove on the end of an empty arm.

"Oh here is it!" He gently pulled out the oboe from where it had been tucked beside him, and handed it to her.

She began to play an improvised melody. A tune of sunlight, and space, and escapes. A tune of the joy of sadness, and the melancholy of hope. A tune of beaches, and ships, and billions of orbiting rocks.

Colin smiled as he listened. Hannah played out the melody, then paused, and lowered the oboe. She slumped over, leaning her head on Colin's shoulder, and closed her eyes.

Again the asteroid belt lay ahead. They had been through it before, but this time it felt different. This time it was not merely a loading zone, a job site. This time it was the hope of a new home, a new start. This time it was a jumping off point in an unending zone of uncountable rocks, with myriad outposts, filled with infinite possibilities.

Author's Note

Thanks so much for reading my book. I hope you enjoyed it! Please consider leaving a review on Goodreads. This is a huge help to get the word out for a new author like myself.
https://www.goodreads.com/book/show/46805397-symphony-of-destruction

As you may have guessed, this story isn't over. The Spindown Saga continues, following our friends Hannah and Colin, and Brother Anderson as their adventures only get wilder.

To keep to date, join my mailing list:
http://dimensionfold.com/authors/ken/